Ghosts
on the *Coast:*
A Visit to Savannah and the Low Country

Also by Jane R. Wood

Voices in St. Augustine

Adventures on Amelia Island:
A Pirate, A Princess, and Buried Treasure

Trouble on the St. Johns River

To Derek & Alex —
Read the book, then come
check out the ghost
stories for yourself!

Ghosts
on the *Coast:*

A Visit to Savannah and the Low Country

Jane R. Wood

Jane R Wood
12/2/2009

Florida Kids Press, Inc. ◆ Jacksonville, FL

Publisher's Cataloging-In-Publication Data

(Prepared by The Donohue Group, Inc.)

Wood, Jane R., 1947-
Ghosts on the coast : a visit to Savannah and the Low Country / Jane R. Wood.
p. : ill. ; cm.
Includes bibliographical references.
Interest age level: 009-014.
ISBN: 978-0-9792304-6-2

1. Savannah (Ga.)—History—Juvenile fiction. 2. Charleston (S.C.)—History—Juvenile fiction. 3. Pawleys Island (S.C.)—History—Juvenile fiction. 4. Cities and towns—Southern States—History, Local—Juvenile fiction. 5. Cities and towns—Southern States—Social life and customs—Juvenile fiction. 6. Savannah (Ga.)—History—Fiction. 7. Charleston—History—Fiction. 8. Pawleys Island (S.C.)—History—Fiction. 9. Cities and towns—Southern States—History, Local—Fiction. 10. Cities and towns—Southern States—Social life and customs—Fiction. I. Title.

PS3573.O59 G45 2010
813/.6   2009936236

Library of Congress Control Number: 2009936236

Cover design and graphic design by Elizabeth A. Blacker.

Published through:
Florida Kids Press, Inc., 11802 Magnolia Falls Drive
Jacksonville, FL 32258
904-268-9572

Printed and bound in the USA
by United Graphics Incorporated, Mattoon, Illinois.

To Terry Wood who makes it all possible.

*To Elizabeth Blacker who works her
magic on me and my books.*

*To Joe and Manning Lee for introducing
me to the Low Country and The Grey Man.*

Acknowledgements

I love history, so writing this book was a delight. In doing my research in Savannah, Charleston and Pawleys Island, I encountered many people who were very helpful in providing information which I could use in my story. They included tour guides, inn keepers, restaurant staff, store managers, market vendors, museum guides, family historians, and local residents. Southern hospitality is alive and well in these cities!

I must give special thanks to Joe and Manning Lee, residents of Pawleys Island, who filled me with stories of their area, and then took me to visit many of those places. They were a constant source of information and support. They also connected me with Dave Geney, who taught me the finer points of crabbing. Thanks to all of them for giving life to my story and ammunition for Bobby's close encounter with danger and the Grey Man.

I am deeply grateful to Gena Acito who provided editing expertise, and Dickie Anderson who did a content review and helped bring clarity where it was needed. Linda Smigaj, a National Board Certified in Literary teacher, used her years of classroom experience to help me keep young readers engaged in the story.

I also appreciate the support I received from the members of the Jacksonville Freelance Writers' Group. Our monthly meetings keep me connected with other creative minds.

Not enough praise can be given to Elizabeth Blacker, my graphic designer and good friend. I can always rely on her creativity and high standards to make my books look good.

And last, and certainly not least, is my husband, Terry Wood. None of my books would be a reality without his support and encouragement. Every author should be so lucky to have a partner like mine!

Chapter 1
Sounds in the Cemetery

As Joey walked through the cemetery he had a strange feeling he was being followed. He looked over his shoulder several times and did a quick glance across the graveyard, but there was no one there.

This is ridiculous, he thought. *It's broad daylight and my mom and brother and little sister are not far away. Besides, I'm 14 and that's too old to be spooked in a graveyard in the middle of the day. It must be my imagination.*

Then he heard it. A low moaning sound came from behind one of the larger tombstones. At first it sounded like someone was hurt, but then it grew louder with heavy breathing.

This is not good, he thought. *Am I hearing voices or could it really be a ghost? Savannah is supposed to be one of the most haunted cities in America.*

He looked around for his family, but they were no-where in sight. All he could see were dozens of old graves and tombstones, many of them hundreds of years old. The Spanish moss hanging from the branches of the ancient oak trees looked like ghostly shapes hovering over his head. He decided it was time to rejoin his family.

Just then, he heard a twig snap behind him and he spun around to see a figure crouched behind a large marble memorial. His 10-year-old brother Bobby jumped up and said, "Boo!"

"Scared you!" Bobby said with a wide grin.

"No, you did NOT scare me," Joey said in disgust.

"Yeah, I did. I can tell. You're white as a ghost yourself. Wait till I tell Mom and Katy."

"Yeah, well just wait till I tell Mom that you were lurking around this historic site being a prankster," Joey said.

"You can tell her anything you want," Bobby said. "But you and I both know you were scared out of your wits. You actually thought there was something there."

"There was something there all right, only it was a silly kid who should show more respect for the dead."

Bobby was quiet as he looked around.

"You know, I bet all these dead people kinda like it when someone has a little fun in here. Someone's got to liven this place up," he laughed. "Get it, liven it up?"

"That is a sick joke," Joey said. "I hope you're not going

to act this silly for the rest of the weekend."

Before Bobby could respond, their mother called to them. She enjoyed visiting historic places and was excited about sharing Savannah's legends and stories with her kids. Bobby and Joey joined her and 5-year-old Katy under a huge oak tree that shaded several large vaults. They looked like old king-size beds with red-brick headboards.

Jennifer Johnson was one of those mothers who liked to make all their vacations educational. "This is known as the Colonial Park Cemetery," she said. "It was started in 1750 and has more than 9,000 graves here."

"Whoa!" Bobby said. "That's like a little city."

"It actually had to be expanded several times to accommodate all the graves," she said. "Savannah endured many wars and natural disasters throughout its history, including the American Revolution, the Civil War, several bad hurricanes, two major fires, and two yellow fever epidemics. Over there I read a marker that says nearly 700 people died in 1820 during one of those epidemics. Many of them are buried right here."

The kids grew solemn as they looked around at the dozens of graves surrounding them.

"It's hard to read some of the markers," Katy said. "This reminds me of the Huguenot Cemetery we saw in St. Augustine."

"Very good, Katy," her mother said. "That one was built a little later than this one, and it was created for a very different reason. The Huguenot Cemetery was built for Protestants who were forbidden from being buried within the city walls of St. Augustine which was a Catholic city at that time. This cemetery allowed all groups to be buried here – Protestants, Catholics, Jews, Negroes, rich, poor, even strangers."

They wandered down several of the walkways and read a few of the historical markers which told about important events and individuals who had contributed to Georgia's history. Katy was getting tired and said she was thirsty.

"Okay troops, let's go. I have another place I want you to see while we're in this neighborhood. Then we're going to take one of the trolley tours. We'll get something to drink before we get on the trolley."

As they walked out through the arched granite entrance, Bobby whispered to Joey, "You know, this is a popular place. People are dying to go here."

Joey rolled his eyes. "Mom would kill you if she heard you talking like that."

"Well, at least I'm in the right place," he said with a smirk. "They wouldn't have to go far to bury me."

Chapter 2
A Romantic Ghost

The kids followed their mother down Oglethorpe Avenue, one of Savannah's busiest thoroughfares. The street was divided by a landscaped island of massive oak trees, magnolia trees and azalea bushes. Several memorials and historical markers were also visible under the canopy of trees.

They walked past numerous beautifully restored old homes. Many of them had flower boxes with colorful blossoms and lush greenery spilling over the edges. Some had ivy growing up the sides of their walls, making them look like they had been there for a long, long time.

Most of the homes were 4-story structures with the main entrances on the second floor. Decorative staircases led to the front doors. Their mother explained that the main living area was usually on the second floor to help keep the dust and dirt to a minimum before the streets were paved.

"I love these old homes," Katy said. "They look like

something out of the movies. Do famous people live in them?"

"Savannah does have some famous residents, but mostly these are owned by private citizens who have restored these old beauties," her mother said. She went on to tell them about a group of ladies who raised a fuss in the 1950s when one of the old houses was about to be torn down.

"They rescued it the day before it was to be destroyed and raised more than $20,000 to save it from the wrecking ball. That was the beginning of the Historic Savannah Foundation which buys old buildings and sells them to people who want to renovate them."

The kids were silent as they walked. They were used to their mother's historical commentaries. After she told them some of the background on these buildings, they looked at them with a new sense of appreciation.

"You see kids, all through history people have had to take a stand to defend something they feel is worth saving. In this case, it was seven feisty ladies who wanted to preserve the unique architecture that existed here. If they hadn't gotten involved, much of this would have been lost." She waved her hands through the air, indicating the buildings on both sides of the street.

"Mom, how do you know all of this stuff?" Bobby asked.

"History is one of my favorite subjects," she said. "I always read about a place before visiting it. I bought a travel guide and checked out a few books from the library."

She stopped in front of a 4-story pinkish building on the corner of Bull Street.

"Here we are," she said. "This house is Savannah's first National Historic Landmark. Katy, I especially wanted you to see this place. This is the birthplace of Juliette Gordon Low, the founder of the Girl Scouts."

"Oh no," Bobby said. "You're not going to make us take a tour. I don't want to see a bunch of girl stuff."

"Hush," his mother replied. "No, we're not going to take a tour of this house, but I wanted Katy to see it because she might want to be a Girl Scout when she gets a little older. We'll come back and take the tour some other day."

"Just you and me," Katy said, as she stuck her tongue out at Bobby.

"Fine with me," he replied. "Old buildings don't do anything for me."

Just then an excited group of Girl Scouts exited the house. They were chattering and giggling as they walked past the Johnson family.

"That was a great tour," one red-headed girl said. "I

especially liked seeing some of her artwork. She was a good artist."

"I liked the part about the ghost," another girl said. "It's such a romantic story."

As soon as they were out of earshot, Bobby said, "Did she say ghost?"

Katy took a step back away from the building and slipped her hand into her mother's. Jennifer Johnson took a deep breath and chose her words carefully.

"Savannah is considered one of the most haunted cities in the country. In fact, the people here like to tell their ghost stories. I imagine it's good for tourism." She paused, trying to find the right words to explain about the ghost without scaring her 5-year-old daughter.

"The story goes like this. When Juliette Gordon Low's mother died upstairs, two different people say they saw the ghost of her dead husband in the house that day. Because the couple had been very devoted to each other, the family felt Captain Gordon was simply coming to escort his wife to heaven."

"So he was a good ghost?" Katy said in a whisper.

Jennifer looked at Joey and then at Bobby. They knew not to make any comments that could upset their little sister. Bobby pulled his fingers across his lips like he was zipping them shut.

"Yes, I guess he was a good ghost," she replied. "But remember, these are just stories. And you're probably going to hear a lot of them in these old Southern towns. It's part of what makes them interesting, don't you think?"

No one answered. Then Bobby said, "Know what I think? It's time to get something to drink. I'm thirsty and hot and tired!"

"Okay, let's get a snack and then we'll take the trolley tour. That's the next thing on my 'To Do' List. There's a lot of wonderful history in this town and I want you kids to learn about it."

Bobby whispered to Joey, "You can keep the history. Now ghosts, that's another thing. I could get into some serious ghost stories."

"Are you sure you want to go there?" Joey said, as they walked back to their mini-van.

"Go there? Heck, I want to see one. Now that would make a great essay when I go back to school. *What I Saw on My Summer Vacation.* Yeah, seeing a ghost is definitely on my 'To Do' List."

Chapter 3
A Trolley Tour

"Ladies and gentlemen, welcome to Savannah," the driver of the trolley greeted the tourists as they drove away from the visitors center. "For the next 90 minutes, we're going to travel through more than two square miles of one of America's most historic cities."

As the driver maneuvered through the crowded streets, she talked about how the city was laid out in 1733 by General James Oglethorpe, the founder of the city.

"Oglethorpe made a grid of streets and placed 24 city squares strategically throughout the city. Twenty-one of them still exist today, adding to Savannah's picturesque charm. These squares are small parks in the middle of busy neighborhoods, providing residents and visitors a natural oasis where one can rest for a moment on a park bench and enjoy Mother Nature. You'll notice that most of the squares have fountains and statues, not to mention the ancient oak and magnolia trees which provide welcome shade to our steamy Southern climate."

One square in particular caught Joey's interest. It was Wright Square and the tour guide told them about Tomochichi, a Yamacraw Indian chief, who was buried there. A large boulder marked his grave and stood as a tribute to the man who welcomed Oglethorpe and the first settlers. He helped them select the site for their new city, picking a bluff overlooking the river. Many of the early settlers in America were met with hostility from the Native Americans, but that was not the case in Savannah, she explained.

They passed several historic churches, the Colonial Park

Cemetery which they had visited earlier, the Juliette Gordon Low House, and many more mansions and restored homes including the Davenport House. The tour guide told them the same story their mother had shared with them earlier about the seven ladies who saved it from destruction.

"Thanks to them, more than 1,000 homes and buildings have been saved and restored," she said. "The Historic District of Savannah would look very different today if it hadn't been for them."

Then they drove down a curved bumpy road which led to River Street along the Savannah River. The guide told them the large stones in the street were ballast from the sailing ships that came to Savannah in its early trading days.

"What's ballast?" Bobby asked.

His mother explained that large stones were often placed in the holds of empty ships coming to Savannah to weigh them down and keep them stable. As the ships were loaded with crops and products for export, the stones were thrown out along the waterfront. These large round stones were then used to pave the streets, build walls and even buildings.

"Sounds like early recycling to me," Joey said with a laugh.

A lady from New York asked several questions about the

different architectural styles. The driver explained that because Savannah was so prosperous in its early years many people became wealthy. Some of them built large mansions reflecting their personal tastes, which is why there were so many different styles. She suggested her visitors stroll through some of the streets and squares to truly appreciate the diversity of the city's buildings.

"Many of these houses are open for tours," she added.

Another lady who was dressed in black asked about the ghosts.

"Oh, we do have our ghosts," the guide answered. "If you're interested, you can take one of our ghost tours. They're walking tours that take place at night."

Bobby turned in his seat and looked pleadingly at his mother.

"Don't even think about it!" she said. "We'll do that another time when you-know-who is a little older."

Katy gave him a teasing grin and batted her eyelashes. Bobby turned around with a deep sigh.

Jennifer tapped Bobby on the shoulder. He ignored her for a moment as he pouted, but then his brother elbowed him to turn around.

"How would you like to go to The Pirates' House for dinner? I know you don't like old buildings, but this one is rather unique. They say it was a favorite hangout for pirates, and there's even a tunnel underneath the building that goes from the restaurant straight to the river. The pirates would shanghai unsuspecting souls who would wake up the next day aboard a ship far out at sea."

The kids were spellbound. She told them some of the scenes described in the book *Treasure Island* were supposed to have taken place in that very building. Robert Louis Stevenson, the author of *Treasure Island*, mentions Savannah several times in the book.

"Rumor has it that Captain Flint, the one who buried the treasure in *Treasure Island*, died in one of the upstairs rooms. 'Darby, bring aft the rum' is said to be his last words," their mother said.

"I read that book last year in 8th grade," Joey said. "This is cool! Let's go."

"Bobby, does that sound like some place you'd like to go or should we find a McDonalds?" his mother asked.

"The Pirates' House works for me," Bobby said. "Do they have regular people food or do we have to eat what the pirates ate?"

"It's a favorite place among tourists so I'm sure they have regular food."

"Then shiver me timbers, what are we waiting

for?" Bobby said.

Katy pulled on her mother's sleeve. "Boys are silly," she said. "Next time let's leave them at home."

"You got it! We'll do a girl trip next time," her mother replied.

Chapter 4
The Pirates' House

A waiter placed menus in front of each of them after they were seated in the Buccaneer's Room. The kids' menus were written on paper that could be made into a pirate's hat.

The room had heavy wooden beams in the ceiling with old lanterns hanging from the rafters. Some of the walls were made of old bricks that looked like they had been there for centuries. Other walls were made of wood and had windows and doors which led to additional dining areas. In one corner a staircase led down to a lower level, but a sign on a gate in front of it said "None shall pass beyond this point...OR ELSE!!!"

"Welcome to The Pirates' House. My name is Elijah and I'm going to be taking care of you. May I get you something to drink?" the waiter said.

"Bring me my rum," Bobby said, imitating Captain Flint.

Joey rolled his eyes. Katy put her elbows on the table and just stared at him. Jennifer looked at the waiter and shook her head.

The waiter addressed Bobby and said very seriously, "Sir, I'm so sorry but our ration of rum has not yet arrived from the islands. May I serve you a chilled glass of lemonade instead?"

Bobby replied with a dramatic sigh, "I guess that will have to do." Then he picked up his menu and began to examine his choices.

Jennifer smiled at the waiter and ordered iced tea for herself and lemonade for Katy. Joey asked for a soft drink.

After the waiter left with their drink order, Joey said, "Bobby, you embarrassed all of us. Don't be such a smart aleck."

"I'm just trying to have some fun. Besides, I was showing my literary expertise."

Their mother reached across the table and touched both boys on their arms. In a serious tone she reminded them they were on vacation and this was supposed to be a fun time for all of them. If they continued to bicker, it would not be fun for her.

She looked both boys in the eyes and waited for a response. Bobby mumbled he was sorry, and Joey said he'd try to ignore his stupid brother. When Bobby started to respond to Joey's insult, Jennifer gave him a stern look and suggested they read some of the history of the building which was printed on the menus.

The menu explained that an experimental garden was created on that exact spot when the early settlers first arrived. The colonists had brought seeds, cuttings, and plants from around the world to see which would thrive in this area. Many of the crops failed due to weather and soil conditions, but products like cotton and peaches were very successful. Cotton became known as white gold for many years and contributed greatly to the economic success of

Savannah. Georgia is still known today for its delicious peaches.

A small structure called The Herb House, said to be the oldest house in Georgia, was built on that plot of land in 1734. This small building was incorporated into the restaurant and now serves as an additional dining room.

When the waiter returned with their drinks, he asked if they had any questions.

"Were there really pirates here in this very room?" Katy said warily.

"Yes, ma'am. When Savannah became a thriving seaport, they built an inn here. Inns also served food and drink

so it became a gathering place for sailors and pirates," he said. "See that fenced off area over there?"

They all turned to look to the corner of the room.

"That goes to the rum cellar and a tunnel that leads to the river. There are stories about men who came here for a friendly drink and ended up in far distant places," he said. "I'll take your food order and tell you about the ghosts after you eat."

Katy looked at her mother for reassurance. Joey looked at Elijah, trying to decide whether to take him seriously. And Bobby said, "Cool. I'll have a cheeseburger."

The rest of them ordered. Joey said to Bobby, "Why did you order a hamburger when we're in a town known for its seafood?"

"I need a big juicy burger in case I run into any ghosts. Someone's got to protect the womenfolk. And I'll be ready!"

"Oh, good grief," Joey said. Their mother just shook her head.

Chapter 5
Ghostly Images

Jennifer reminded her kids they would probably hear many colorful stories, and they needed to keep them in perspective. Joey asked his mother if it was okay for him to look at the framed pages of some of the early editions of *Treasure Island* that were hanging on the wall. Jennifer said yes to Joey, but no to Bobby when he said he wanted to go check out the rum cellar.

When their food arrived, Elijah said he'd let them enjoy their dinner but would be back to tell them about the spirits who reside there. Bobby took a big bite of his burger and announced this was now his favorite restaurant. He told them he would buy a restaurant some day near a river or the ocean and he'd have all his waiters dress up as pirates.

"Maybe I'll throw in a ghost or two," he said.

Joey wanted to comment, but knew it would only start trouble so he took a bite of his crab cake sandwich and focused on his French fries. The restaurant was getting crowded and many tourists kept walking through the dining room.

Elijah returned and encouraged them to check out the different dining areas in the restaurant before they left. He told them more about the early history of the tavern and inn which is now considered a house museum.

"Tell us about the ghosts," Bobby said. "Have you seen any yourself?"

"I haven't seen any, but I've heard a few," he said. "And many of the other workers here have seen them. Actually, I did take a picture of one though.

"A friend of mine wanted some photos taken with her digital camera, so I said I'd shoot some when the place was empty. When we enlarged one of the pictures and studied it closely, we could see a distinct image of a pirate."

"For real?" Bobby said.

"For real," he said. "After that, I was convinced they're here. Rumor has it that Captain Flint died upstairs. They say he haunts the place on moonless nights."

"Okay, that's enough for now," Jennifer said, pushing her salad bowl away. She nodded her head toward Katy who was looking around furtively. Elijah got the message.

"Would anyone like dessert?" he asked.

"No, I think we're done," Jennifer said. "I thought we'd walk along River Street later and visit one of the candy stores. That will be enough sugar for this crew," she said.

Before they left, they checked out several of the other rooms. A young lady dressed like a pirate wench was giving tours. They joined one of the groups and learned more about the history of the building and its pirates and ghosts. Joey took several pictures with his digital camera.

"Do you think you got any ghosts in your shots?" Bobby asked Joey quietly.

"If I did, you'll be the first to know," he replied. Joey was thinking the same thing and was anxious to check out the photos later. He knew when he downloaded them onto his computer he could enlarge them and would be able to examine them closely.

Capturing a ghost in one of the pictures would really make Bobby's essay on what he saw during his summer vacation more dramatic, he thought and chuckled to himself.

As they walked to their van, Katy asked if it was going to be a moonless night.

"No, I think we've got a full moon tonight," Joey said. "But don't worry about a thing. There won't be any ghosts at our motel." He winked at his mother.

"OK, but just in case, we'd better sleep with a light on tonight," Katy said.

They all agreed that would be a good idea.

Chapter 6
River Street

Their motel was located in the Historic District so they were able to walk to River Street that evening. It was much cooler now that the sun had gone down.

They walked past souvenir shops, restaurants, gift shops, inns, and specialty stores with all kinds of items including clothing, jewelry, art, gourmet food items and books. The sidewalk was narrow, so many people spilled onto the cobblestone street despite the traffic. Jennifer insisted Katy hold someone's hand as they walked.

A triple-decker paddlewheel boat was leaving the dock for its nightly dinner cruise. Katy waved to some of the passengers who were standing on the front deck.

"Maybe we can do that when we come back," she said to her mother.

"Sounds like fun," her mother replied.

They walked through several of the souvenir shops. Bobby identified several things he'd like to have, but he was reluctant to spend any of his allowance money. Their mother had said earlier they'd be visiting a candy store, so he decided to save his money to satisfy his sweet tooth.

When they entered the candy store, Bobby knew instantly it was worth the wait. The first things he saw were dozens of caramel apples in a glass display case. Some of the apples were plain; some were covered with nuts; and others were coated with chocolate and multi-colored sprinkles.

Katy was drawn to the large colorful barrels that contained individually wrapped candies of all varieties. "Look, Mom," she exclaimed. "It looks like a rainbow of candies.

I've never seen so many different kinds in one place."

Joey zeroed in on the fudge and pralines. "Grandma would love this place," he said when his mother joined him. "The whole place smells like chocolate."

Jennifer let the kids explore and check out all the display cases, shelves laden with candy jars, and pre-packaged bags and boxes. She knew it was just a matter of time before they popped the question. And she was ready.

"Each of you may spend $5.00. My treat. You may save your allowance money for something else. We've got the rest of the week and there will be other things you'll want to buy with your money."

"What if I want more than $5.00 worth?" Bobby asked. "Can I spend some of my money too?"

"You don't need more than $5.00 worth of candy, young man. You'll be bouncing off the walls tonight from a sugar high," she said.

Bobby frowned and wandered off to make a difficult decision. Joey said he wanted some dark chocolate fudge with nuts and offered to share it with his mother, as he knew she loved dark chocolate.

"Get what you want, Joey. I intend to spend $5.00 on myself," she said with a wink and a grin.

"OK, then I'm going for the pralines. I can taste them

already," he said as he smacked his lips.

Katy was filling a plastic zip bag with a variety of wrapped candies. She spent several minutes looking at all the candies before she dropped some into her bag.

"My favorite ones are the kinds that get fizzy. It feels like sparkles in my mouth," she told Joey who came to help her.

When everyone had made their choices, Jennifer paid a young man in an apron who had been stirring a large copper pot of caramel for the apples. She also bought a tin of glazed pecans for their grandparents as a thank-you gift for taking care of Max, their dog, while they were gone.

"I know Grandma would love some chocolate, but it would melt before we got it home. Your grandfather likes pecans. This will have to do. Maybe we can find something else for them later in the trip," she said, but no one was listening.

They were all enjoying their after-dinner treats. She grabbed a few napkins as they left the store.

Chapter 7
The Waving Girl

Jennifer steered the kids across the street to Riverfront Plaza, a brick walkway that ran along the waterfront. As they strolled along, she started one of her 'Mom tours' again.

James Oglethorpe was very smart to pick this location for his new colony, she told them. The Savannah River has contributed greatly to the city's success. She pointed out that the same buildings along River Street which contain shops and restaurants today were once warehouses which provided easy access to the river. That meant ship transportation to markets all over the world, she explained.

"Cotton was grown on many of the surrounding plantations and became a source of much of Georgia's wealth. Eli Whitney actually invented the cotton gin on a plantation near here," she said.

"How did Georgia get its name?" Katy asked.

"It was named after King George II who was the king of England at that time."

Bobby announced that if he ever started a city, he would name it Bobby Town. "No, better yet, I'll call it Port Bobby, because I want it to be along a river so I can build my restaurant there. Remember, the one where all the waiters will dress up as pirates?" he said to Joey.

"Yeah, I remember," Joey said sarcastically.

They strolled toward the eastern end of River Street and stopped in front of a life-size statue of a girl and a dog.

"Who's Florence Martus?" Joey asked, after reading the name at the base of the statue. "And why is she waving that cloth?"

A lady who was sitting on one of the benches near the statue answered his question.

"That is The Waving Girl," she said matter-of-factly. "As a young girl, Florence would wave at the passing ships. During the day she would wave a cloth and when it got dark she waved a lantern. The sailors on the ships would wave back and often return her greeting with a blast of their ship's horn. She continued to do it for 44 years, well into adulthood. They figured she welcomed more than 50,000 ships in the early 1900s."

The woman paused to pop a peanut in her mouth. She was shelling peanuts and collecting the shells in a neat row on the bench beside her. Occasionally she'd throw one to a nearby squirrel. She swallowed and continued.

"I moved here in 1972, the year this statue was created, so I feel a special kinship to Florence. She died in 1943, and that same year they christened a Liberty ship in her honor."

"What's a Liberty ship?" Bobby asked his mother.

"Those were cargo ships built in the United States during World War II to carry war supplies to troops throughout the Atlantic and Pacific Oceans. Some were named after war heroes and famous leaders, but many were named after regular citizens as a tribute to things they had done."

"You'll study World War II when you get to middle school," Joey said to Bobby. "Our history teacher told us some of the Liberty ships were built in Jacksonville. That's where we live," he said to the lady on the bench.

"I think it's cool they named one of those ships after a woman," Katy said.

The peanut lady said, "They actually named many of them after women and some after African-Americans, which was quite an honor back then."

Jennifer suggested they all pose for a picture in front of the statue. She said one of them might want to do a report on the Liberty ships some day and a photo taken here could come in handy. Katy said she would do her report on

Florence Martus.

"I like to hear about women who make a difference," Katy said.

"Remember the story about Anna Kingsley, the African slave who ended up owning the plantation she had lived and worked on," Joey said.

"Yeah, and Kate Bailey who wouldn't let the city workers cut down a big oak tree in front of her house on Amelia Island," Katy said. "She was awesome!"

"And what about the ladies we heard about today who saved that building," her mother said. "Many women have left their mark on history."

The woman on the bench agreed. "In my day, women were only expected to be nurses or teachers or secretaries. Today a young lady can do anything she wants. Now we have women doctors, women generals, women pilots, even women astronauts. Yes indeed, it's a great time for a young girl to be growing up today. The whole world is open to you," she said to Katy.

Katy smiled at her and said, "Yes, ma'am."

Jennifer thanked the woman for explaining the background of The Waving Girl to her kids. "Time to head back to the motel," she said. "We have a busy day tomorrow."

As a large container ship sailed by, Katy jumped up and down and waved her bag of candy in the air. To her delight one of the sailors walking along the deck of the vessel stopped, gave a crisp salute to her, and waved back.

"Way to go, Katy," Joey said. "Maybe you'll get a statue some day too."

"Hah, I'd rather have a ship named after me. The Katy Johnson! How does that sound?"

"I like it," Joey said.

"Me, too," she said, and slipped a sticky hand into one of his as they followed their mother back to the motel.

Chapter 8
A Christmas Present for Abraham Lincoln

The next day the weather was hot and humid. Bobby complained that he didn't feel like walking around in the heat. The others agreed. Jennifer said there were a few other places she wanted to see, but they could drive by them and then they'd head to Charleston.

She drove down Broughton Street which looked like the downtown area of many older American cities. Tourists and many young adults were meandering in and out of the shops and restaurants. Jennifer told the kids the Savannah College of Art and Design owned buildings all throughout the city, which explained all the college students.

"I like to draw," Katy said. "Maybe I could go here some day."

Jennifer pulled into a parking space across the street from The Marshall House.

"That was the first hotel in Savannah and it was built before the Civil War. During the war it was occupied by

Union troops led by General Sherman. Joey, did you study about Sherman's March to the Sea in your American history class?" she asked.

"Was he the one who had the scorched earth policy?" Joey said.

"Yes," she said and before she could go on, Bobby spoke up.

"Wait a minute," Bobby interrupted. "When was the Civil War and what does scorched earth mean?"

Jennifer told them the Civil War occurred in the 1860s and is also known as the War Between the States.

"It was when the Southern states, which relied heavily

on slaves to work their plantations, decided they wanted to break away from the Northern states. They were opposed to many of the policies that were being imposed on them by the government, so they formed the Confederate States of America."

She explained that President Abraham Lincoln was against slavery. He considered their secession from the Union as an act of rebellion, which is why they were called the rebels. When some of the Confederate forces attacked a U.S. military installation at Fort Sumter in South Carolina, the Civil War began. She told them they'd see Fort Sumter when they visited Charleston.

"It was a terrible time in our country's history and a very deadly war. Soldiers from Southern states were fighting against soldiers from Northern states, sometimes against their own relatives," she said. The mini-van was very quiet.

"So what was the scorched earth policy?" Bobby asked again.

"William Tecumseh Sherman was a Union general who burned large parts of the city of Atlanta and then marched his troops eastward to the sea, burning everything in its path. As you can imagine, this was a terrible blow to the Confederacy and helped lead to their defeat.

"However, when he got here – and this is an interesting part of Savannah's history – the city leaders did not want their beautiful city destroyed, so they surrendered to him. Savannah was captured in late December in 1864. General Sherman sent a message to President Lincoln offering Savannah to him as a Christmas present. The war ended shortly afterward."

"And his soldiers stayed in that hotel?" Katy said, pointing to the 4-story structure across the street. It had an iron veranda that ran the entire length of the second floor.

"Yes," her mother replied. "Near the end of the war, they made it in to a hospital for the wounded troops. They say there's a Union soldier who still haunts the place."

"You mean a ghost?" Bobby exclaimed.

"That's what they say," she replied. "And there's another story about a little girl ghost who likes to tickle guests' feet."

Bobby chuckled and even Katy smiled.

"She must be a playful ghost," Katy said.

"This hotel also has the distinction of being the home of the man who wrote the *Uncle Remus* stories. You know, the Br'er Rabbit stories I used to read to you?"

"I like Br'er Rabbit," Bobby said. "He is always playing tricks on the other characters in the stories. He's my hero!"

Jennifer laughed. "I'm glad you remember something from all those stories I read to you at bedtime."

She studied the city map in her travel guide and then eased the mini-van back into the morning traffic. She told them she had some more buildings she wanted to see and then they'd be off to Charleston.

Chapter 9
Lafayette Square

Joey helped his mother navigate her way to Lafayette Square. They turned on Abercorn Street, driving past the Colonial Park Cemetery again.

Bobby, who was sitting in the back seat with his sister, whispered to her, "People are dying to go there."

She gave him a very serious look at first, and then started to giggle. Joey looked over his shoulder from the front seat and gave Bobby a disgusted look.

"What?" Bobby said.

"You know what," he replied.

As they approached Lafayette Square, they saw a beautiful cathedral on the corner. The massive white structure had two towering spires that reached heavenward.

"Oh wow!" Katy said. "It's beautiful."

"This is one of the buildings I wanted to see," her mother said. "Let me park and we can walk over to the square."

She found a parking space on one of the side streets

that led into the square. As the kids tumbled out of the van, they knew they were going to get a mini-lesson in architecture, but they didn't mind. They discovered that buildings became more interesting when they knew more about their history and how they were built.

As they walked toward the square, Jennifer began to explain. "That church is the Cathedral of St. John the Baptist and it's an example of French Gothic-style architecture. It was first erected in the 1870s, destroyed by a fire in 1898, and re-built in the 1900s. From the pictures I've seen, it's magnificent inside. I'll visit it on a future trip."

She led them across the street to Lafayette Square and

told them it was named after the Marquis de Lafayette who actually visited there in 1825.

"What's a marquis and why was he important?" Bobby asked.

"A marquis is a European nobleman. The Marquis de Lafayette was a French military officer who served in the Continental Army with George Washington during the American Revolution. He is honored with monuments in many American cities."

They walked along a brick walkway and stopped in front of the 3-tiered fountain at the square's center. Jennifer swept her arms in a wide circle pointing to the houses and mansions that surrounded them.

"Mom, you really get into old buildings, don't you?" Joey said.

She nodded. "The architectural style of the buildings often reflects the era in which they were constructed and the personal preferences of the owners. Remember the tour guide yesterday told us Savannah is known for its wide variety of styles.

"For example, over there is the Andrew Low House," she said, pointing to a cream-colored house with green shutters. "He was the husband of Juliette Gordon Low, the founder of the Girl Scouts. We saw her birthplace yesterday. She lived here after she was married. That house is known for its ironwork balconies." They studied it for a few minutes.

She then directed their attention to a brick house across

the street which looked very different from all the others.

"You'll see many homes like that later today when we get to Charleston," she said. "The main entrance to the house is on the side through a 2-story veranda. The house may look very plain from the street, but that can be misleading. They can be full of Southern charm inside."

Then she pointed to a 3-story house on the same block.

"That was the childhood home of Flannery O'Connor. She was a famous Southern writer. You'll probably read some of her stories in school. That house looks rather plain next to some of the other grander homes here.

"Bobby, you'll like this story about Flannery O'Connor," she said. "They say at the age of five she taught a chicken to walk backwards in the garden behind the house."

"You're kidding, right?" Bobby said.

"No, that's what I read in the travel guide."

"Now that's cool. I can't even teach Max to go in a circle and dogs have got to be smarter than chickens," he said. "Can we get a chicken when we get home?"

"No, absolutely not," she said. "But follow me. I've got another story I think you'll like."

Chapter 10
A Grand Victorian Lady

Jennifer walked them across the street and stopped in front of a large 3-story house located at 330 Abercorn Street. The vanilla-colored mansion had tall windows with four decorative ironwork balconies across the front.

"This is the one I really wanted to see," she said, looking at it longingly. "It's the Hamilton-Turner House which is now an inn. It's called the 'Grand Victorian Lady' and some day I want to stay there."

She stood there for a few moments not saying anything, just drinking in all its features. She told her kids it was the first house in Savannah to have electricity and that it escaped the horrible fire that burned down the cathedral one block away because it had a tin roof.

"This is a classic style of architecture made popular in France, but it also has some Victorian features," Jennifer told them.

She pointed out the molds over the windows, the

painted trim across the façade, and the elegant portico giving it a grand entrance. When she got her camera out and started taking pictures, the kids wandered around the corner to see what was there.

"I hope Mom doesn't expect us to stay there with her," Bobby said. "It doesn't look like a place for kids." And then he added, "Although it does remind me of the Haunted Mansion at Disney World. I wonder if it's haunted."

Just then, Joey heard some giggling coming from inside the house.

"Sounds like those kids are having a good time," Joey said.

"What kids?" Bobby said.

"The ones who are laughing. It sounds like they're playing some kind of game rolling balls across the floor," he replied.

"I don't hear anything," Bobby said.

Joey put his index finger to his lips, signaling them to be quiet, "Listen."

Joey heard more peels of laughter coming from one of the top floors.

"Did you hear that?" he said.

"I don't hear anything! There are no kids in that house. You're just trying to make a fool out of me," Bobby said and stomped away.

Joey looked perplexed. He leaned over the short cast iron fence, looking up and down the side yard, and then walked around toward the back of the house. No kids there. As he walked back to where they had been standing, he saw Katy staring at an open window on the top floor.

"Joey," she said in a very quiet voice. "I heard them too." She looked at him with concern. "How come Bobby didn't hear anything?"

"I dunno, Katy. Maybe Bobby was just teasing us. Let's go ask him."

Bobby was standing next to their mother under a huge magnolia tree on the corner. "Got any good ghost stories to tell about this place?" he said.

Jennifer cleared her throat and glanced around, as if what she was about to say was a big secret. She looked at Katy for a moment, and then started her story.

"One of the books I read about Savannah revealed several ghost stories. Remember now, these are just stories," she said as she looked at Katy. "They say this house is haunted by the ghosts of children who play games on the top floor and can be heard giggling."

Joey took a step backward and stumbled off the sidewalk into the street. Katy threw her hand to her mouth, and

Bobby went running around to the side of the house.

"What's going on?" Jennifer demanded. Katy and Joey looked at each other in disbelief.

"We heard them," Katy said. "Joey and I heard the giggles."

"Oh, come on now. I'm sure there's a logical explanation for what you heard."

"I don't know," Joey said. "It sure sounded like kids and it seemed like it was coming from the top floor."

He gave his mother a knowing look. They were both remembering the time he heard voices in St. Augustine, but could never explain where they came from.

"Mom, this time Katy heard them too," he added. "But Bobby didn't. At least he said he didn't."

The three of them walked around the corner and joined Bobby who was pacing back and forth along the sidewalk. "I still don't hear anything. I thought you guys were making it up and just trying to trick me."

They stood there silently for several minutes just listening, but there was no laughter to be heard. Finally Bobby said he was getting hot and was ready to go.

Joey looked at his mother, realizing they needed some kind of closure for Katy. Before either one of them could say anything, Katy shrugged her shoulders and said, "Well, I guess we'll never know."

Joey grinned. "It will just be another one of our adventures that we'll tell our friends about."

"Let's go, before y'all start seeing things too," Bobby whined. And with that, they left Savannah.

Chapter 11
The Low Country

On the way to Charleston they played the letter game. The object of the game was to find all the letters of the alphabet in alphabetical order on billboards, or signs on restaurants and gas stations. Jennifer offered a banana split to the first one to spot all the letters. Because Katy was 5, she only had to go to the letter "m". She also got to sit in the front seat, making it easier for her to see the signs first.

Once a letter was sighted and claimed by one of them, no one else could use it. There was a lot of chatter every time they approached an exit on the interstate because that's where the most signs were located. Jennifer helped Katy by coughing every time she saw one Katy needed.

As always, Joey and Bobby were competing against each other. They were racing to finish before they turned off of I-95, because they figured there would be fewer signs to read on Highway 17. Joey was stuck on "z" and Bobby was looking for an "x," when Katy yelled "I see an 'm'! I win!"

"That's not fair," Bobby whined. "Mom was helping you."

"Yeah, and I'm going to share my yummy banana split with her," she said with a sassy tone. "You boys can eat crackers and drink water."

"Speaking of eating, is anyone ready for lunch?" Jennifer said.

A chorus of yeses echoed throughout the mini-van. She selected a fast food restaurant she knew they all liked. After lunch, things were much quieter. Bobby rode in the front seat and stared blankly out the window. Joey read a book in the back seat next to Katy who had fallen asleep.

They drove through some heavily wooded areas of pine and oak trees. The road eventually opened up to rural landscapes sprinkled with endless fields, fenced pastures, and an occasional farm house. When they crossed a bridge over an expansive marsh, Jennifer said, "That's why they call this the Low Country."

Bobby studied the countryside for awhile and then said, "I wonder how the early explorers got through all this water. These marshes have got to be loaded with snakes and alligators and tons of mosquitoes. Yuck."

"From what I've read, they learned a lot from the Indians who had lived here for hundreds of years. They knew how to survive," she replied.

"Yeah, but still…there were no roads or maps even. I bet a lot of them died."

"Of course they did. That's why it's important to study history. It gives us an appreciation for those who came before us. Somebody had to pave the way."

Bobby was quiet for the next few miles as they cruised past easy-flowing creeks and soggy marshes. He could see snowy white egrets dotting the landscape, some wading through lazy waters with their long spindly legs while others perched in trees along the water's edge. He spotted an osprey nest high in a pine tree. Other birds which he couldn't identify flew over the marsh grasses looking for their next meal.

"Mom, this is really pretty, isn't it?" he said.

"Yes it is," she said. "I'm glad you like it. And I think you're really going to enjoy Pawleys Island. No more tours or old buildings to look at. The rest of the weekend we're going to enjoy Mother Nature."

As they got closer to Charleston, the road became more congested. Cars and trucks zipped in and out of the parking lots from stores, restaurants, and gas stations that lined the highway.

"I'd like to get to our motel before the rush hour traffic starts. Bobby, will you help me look for signs that direct us to the Historic District?" Jennifer said.

"Sure, I can do that," he said. "Do they have a pool at our motel?"

"Yes, they do. Would you like to go swimming before we do some exploring?"

"Yep. It's hot out there. Swimming is high on my 'To Do' List," he said with a grin.

"Then swimming it is!"

Chapter 12
Cooling Off

While the kids frolicked in the pool, Jennifer flipped through a notebook of restaurant menus she had picked up in the motel lobby. She stretched out on a lounge chair near the shallow end of the pool where she could keep an eye on Katy. Bobby instigated a game of Marco Polo, inviting three kids from North Carolina to play.

"If you're looking for a good kid-friendly restaurant for dinner, we can suggest a few," said the mother of the kids in the pool. "We've been here for three days and have discovered some that have worked out nicely for us."

"Why, thank you," Jennifer replied. "That would be great."

The other woman named several places where they had eaten and gave Jennifer directions to them.

"We're only here for tonight and tomorrow, and then we're going to spend several days at the beach," Jennifer said. "My kids love the ocean. I'm afraid I may have overdosed them on history and architecture in Savannah. I think I'll let them just be kids for the rest of the week. They'll be starting school when we get back, so this is their last hoorah for the summer."

"I know what you mean," the other woman said. "We want our kids to learn as much as they can when we travel. It's hard finding a balance that keeps everyone happy. I'm sure your kids will love the beach."

When the game was over and Bobby started bragging because he had won, the water war began. Mostly it was Joey and Bobby splashing each other, but their new friends also got into the act. Jennifer decided to put a stop to it

© iStockphoto

before someone got hurt.

"I think it's time to get some dinner," she announced to her three kids. Looking at her watch, she said, "The bus is leaving in 20 minutes. Anyone who's going with me better be dressed and ready to go."

Her kids knew the routine. If she said 20 minutes, she meant it. They bounded out of the pool, said their goodbyes to their North Carolina friends, and wrapped themselves in fluffy white towels. Walking back to their room, Bobby stepped on a small pebble in his bare feet and howled like a dog. Joey laughed out loud, but Jennifer stepped between the two of them before a new battle could begin.

Joey raced into the room so he could be first in the bathroom. After three quick showers to wash off the chlorine, they draped their bathing suits over the lawn chairs on the small patio outside their room and boarded their mom's 'bus'.

Chapter 13
Seafood and Sundaes

They drove down Meeting Street toward the Old City Market. Jennifer told them their playmates' mother had suggested several good restaurants in that area. They couldn't find a parking space on the street, so ended up in one of the parking garages. As they walked along Bay Street toward Market Street, Jennifer explained that Charleston's history dated back to the late 1600s.

"Charleston is older than Savannah. The early settlers tried two other locations before establishing a permanent settlement here," she explained. "This city was named after the king of England, who was Charles II at that time."

"A lot of the buildings look old, just like in Savannah," Bobby said.

"They are old. Many cities like to preserve their history, so they have laws to protect the old buildings," she said.

"Yeah, like the ladies in Savannah who saved that house," Katy said.

"And like St. Augustine," Joey added. "I remember they have restrictions on what kinds of changes people can make to buildings that are in the historic district."

"This doesn't happen only in the South," Jennifer told them. "You'll find it's true in New England, out West, and all over the world. Preserving history is important to many communities."

"I like seeing old buildings," Katy said. "And I really like it when people dress up in old-fashioned clothes. Can I get one of those old dresses some day?"

"I've got lots of old clothes you can have," Bobby said.

"Not that kind of old clothes," she said. "I want a long skirt with ruffles and maybe an apron. The ladies always wore aprons, even the young girls."

"Sorry, I don't have a single apron in my closet," Bobby said.

They turned onto Market Street and saw the first of four long open-air markets that extended for several blocks. The brick structures had stalls for dozens of vendors who sold all kinds of souvenirs. Because it was early evening, the market was already closed for the day.

"We can come back here tomorrow, if you'd like. I know you want to spend some of your money, and this might be a good place for you to do that," Jennifer said. "Now let's find a place to eat. I'm ready for some fresh seafood."

They checked out the menus posted in front of several of the restaurants that were on Jennifer's list and finally settled on one that appealed to all of them. A hostess seated them in a crowded dining room and gave Katy and Bobby kids' menus.

"How come you didn't get one of these?" Bobby said to Joey.

"Because I'm not a kid. I'm a full-fledged teenager who eats man-sized portions." He flexed his arm muscles. "I need to maintain my manly figure."

Bobby laughed. "You didn't look very manly last Halloween when you dressed up as an old lady."

Joey blushed. Then he recovered by saying, "Only someone who's very confident with his manhood could do something like that." Then he dramatically opened his menu and said, "And now my baby brother, let me study this fine document and decide what kind of nourishment I shall order."

"I'd like to order you to the dungeon," Bobby said.

Their mother intervened. "Actually, we're going to see a dungeon tomorrow. And if you don't stop bickering, I'm going to leave both of you there. Now cut the chatter and decide what you want to eat."

Katy selected the kids' fish sandwich with fries. Bobby decided on the fried shrimp. Joey wanted to try something he had never had before, so he ordered the blackened grouper. Shrimp and Grits was their mother's choice.

"I've never had it before and I hear it's a specialty of this area," she said.

None of them were disappointed with their dinners. Because of the time they had spent in the pool, the kids had worked up some serious appetites. At the end of the meal Joey declared them all members of the 'clean plate club.' When the waitress asked if they wanted dessert, they looked at their mother longingly.

© iStockphoto

"How about a banana split for the whole table?" she said.

Katy clapped her hands. "It will be MY banana split, and if you're all good, I'll share it with you."

Joey draped his arm around his little sister. "You're my favorite sister in the whole wide world," he said, batting his eyelashes.

"You silly goose, I'm you're only sister," she said.

"Oh, you noticed that. Well, you're still high on my favorite people list."

"Good grief! What some people won't do for a little ice cream," Bobby said.

Soon a monstrous sundae with four spoons was placed in the middle of their table. Everyone let Katy have the first bite. She called dibs on the cherry and scooped it up with a mouthful of whipped cream. It didn't take long for the feasting to begin.

When they were done, Bobby said, "That was outstanding!"

"I couldn't agree with you more, little brother," Joey replied.

"I'm just glad you two finally agree on something," their mother said.

74

Chapter 14
The Holy City

After dinner, Jennifer suggested they walk off their dinner and check out a few of the places she had read about.

"It will be much cooler tonight," she said. "Tomorrow is supposed be another scorcher."

"I can't wait till we get to the beach," Bobby said. "I'm going to stay in the water all day."

"I wanna build a sand castle," Katy said. "I hope they have some buckets and shovels at the place where we're staying."

Jennifer explained they'd be staying in a beach house on Pawleys Island about 70 miles up the coast from Charleston. A friend of hers from college had rented it for a month, but her family had to go to Atlanta this weekend for a wedding, so she offered it to Jennifer for three nights.

"I'm sure they'll have some beach toys," she said.

They walked down Church Street for several blocks. They stopped in front of a large brownish church with huge columns just as a horse-drawn carriage carrying three elderly ladies stopped in front of it. The driver of the carriage began to describe the church.

"Charleston is known as The Holy City," he told them. "This is St. Philips Episcopal Church. This parish was established in 1680, but this building only dates back to 1836. It has weathered many disasters, including hurricanes, fires, a major earthquake, a tornado, and it was even shelled by the Union army during the Civil War."

"Oh, gracious sakes alive!" said one of the ladies with a thick Southern drawl. "Those mean ole Yankees!"

"Yes, ma'am, I understand how you feel," the driver said. "But it was wartime and the Union troops were targeting the steeple. You see, that was an excellent place for the Confederates to watch for Union ships approaching the harbor."

As the carriage drove away, Jennifer explained that the city of Charleston suffered through several attacks even before the American Revolution and the Civil War. They originally located their town here to be better protected from some not-so-friendly Indians, she said.

"Where we're standing is on a peninsula that has rivers on both sides of it, making it much easier to defend. It also made it more convenient for the plantation owners to transport their rice and cotton here using the natural currents of the water."

"That's just like Savannah," Joey said. "They built their city on a river too."

"You got it!" she said. "The early settlements that survived and thrived had to be smart about where they built their towns."

"Are there any ghosts in this church," Bobby asked.

"As a matter of fact, there is one that's kind of sad," she said. "They say there's a ghost of a woman who died in childbirth who has been seen visiting the grave of her stillborn child in the church's cemetery. A photographer even caught an image of her in one of his pictures."

"Joey, quick! Get your camera. Let's take some pictures in the cemetery," Bobby said. "If we get a picture of her, we can sell it and make lots of money."

"I think it's a little dark for taking pictures now," Joey said. "Besides, I don't think Mom is wild about the idea."

Jennifer was already walking away with Katy.

Bobby gave a deep sigh. "I just want to see a real-live ghost."

"Bobby, do you know how silly that sounds?" Joey said. "If it was real-live, it wouldn't be dead so it couldn't be a ghost."

"You can make fun of me all you want. But before this trip is over, I intend to see one. Dead or alive."

In the next block they came to another church. This one was painted white with black trim and had a wrought iron fence separating it from the sidewalk, but no steeple. Jennifer told them it was the Huguenot Church.

"You mean like the cemetery in St. Augustine?" Katy asked.

"Yes, it's the same group. Many French Protestants came here in the 1680s because the French king was taking away religious freedom for non-Catholics," she told them. "According to my travel book, this is the only remaining independent Huguenot church in America today."

"Do they speak French?" Bobby asked.

"No, the services are in English now. However, they do offer a service in French once a year. That would be kind of neat to hear that, wouldn't it," she said.

"Très magnifique!" Joey said, showing off one of the few French phrases he knew. Then he sheepishly added, "My history teacher used to say that all the time."

Katy was looking across the street and waving to someone in a pink-colored building. It had a balcony with a green wrought iron railing extending along the entire second floor.

"Who are you waving to?" Bobby said.

"That lady up there in the red dress," she said. "She was looking at me out the window, up there on the balcony. Didn't you see her?"

"No, I don't see anyone."

Jennifer joined them and looked a little worried.

"That's the Dock Street Theatre and it's the first building in America designed for theatrical performances. There have been several buildings on that spot, including a once-popular hotel, but many of them were destroyed by fire. The City of Charleston has restored the theatre and performances are still held there today."

© iStockphoto

"Maybe you saw one of the actors," Bobby said.

"Yes, I'm sure that's what it was," Jennifer said. "Let's keep moving. I'd like to see one more historic church before it gets any darker. It's just one more block."

As Joey and Katy walked ahead, Bobby tugged on his mother's sleeve.

"You look worried about something. Is everything okay?"

Jennifer quietly told Bobby that she had read about the ghost of a lady who is often seen on the second floor balcony of the Dock Street Theatre.

"Whoa," he said. "You think Katy saw a real ghost?"

"I don't know. I'm sure there's a logical explanation for what she saw," she said. "I hope so anyway."

They walked silently for the next block. When they got to Broad Street, Jennifer directed them to turn right. They saw was a beautiful white church with a tall spire and a clock tower. It was the oldest church building in South Carolina, she said.

She told them the church bells were stolen by the British during the American Revolution. They got them back, but then they were partially destroyed when Sherman visited Charleston during the Civil War, she said. She reminded them about Sherman's March to the Sea which they had learned about in Savannah.

"These guys had to do lots of rebuilding," Joey said. "Fires, wars, hurricanes."

"I remember when this town was hit hard by Hurricane Hugo in 1989. It destroyed many of the buildings and it took years for them to recover. So they're not immune to destruction today. It still happens," she said. "Let's cross over. I want to see if the graveyard is still open."

It was. They wandered through the cemetery, reading the names and dates on many of the tombstones. Bobby quietly asked his mom if she thought there were any ghosts in this graveyard.

"I hope not. I think we've had enough ghost talk for one day," she said. "But I've got a great pirate story I'll tell you about tomorrow. It's pretty gruesome."

"Wicked!" he said. "I can hardly wait."

Chapter 15
Beginnings and Endings

After breakfast they checked out of the motel. They drove to the Charleston Visitor Center to get an overview of all the attractions. Jennifer bought them tickets to watch a 24-minute video called *Forever Charleston*. It echoed many of the things Jennifer had already told them, but the video and old photographs made it more real.

Then they rode down Meeting Street past stores and restaurants and what seemed like hundreds of tourists. After several more blocks, she turned left on one of the side streets and found a parking place along the waterfront.

She suggested they walk along the promenade that provided a good view of the harbor. A cool ocean breeze was welcome relief from the morning heat as they climbed the stairs to the sea wall. Several tour buses were parked along Bay Street and dozens of tourists were listening to a guide describe the beginning of the Civil War.

He directed their attention eastward across the water to

Fort Sumter. He told them Union forces had occupied Fort Sumter even after South Carolina had seceded from the Union. The South demanded they leave, but they refused. On April 12, 1861, South Carolina Confederate troops opened fire on the fort. They bombarded it for two days, eventually causing the Union troops to leave. It became a symbol of Southern resistance and was one of the defining moments of American history because that was the beginning of the Civil War, he said.

He also told them about the *H. L. Hunley*, a submarine used by the Confederates. It was the first submarine used to sink an enemy warship. Unfortunately, the *Hunley* also sank, drowning its crew of eight, he explained.

"I didn't know they had submarines back then," Joey said to his mother.

"Several years ago I remember reading in the newspaper that they had recovered the *Hunley*. Maybe we can find a book about it."

They walked to the tip of the peninsula where Jennifer pointed out where the Ashley River and Cooper River converged to form Charleston Harbor. Behind them across the street was the Battery which had been a fortification for the city during the Civil War. When it was made into a public park, they erected several war memorials and left pieces of artillery there, she said. Bobby asked if he could cross the street to look at the cannons.

They walked over to the park which was shaded by palmetto and giant oak trees. Bobby and Joey went to check out the cannons and Katy asked if she could walk over to the gazebo that was a short distance away. Jennifer found a bench to sit on where she could see both the boys and Katy.

Soon Bobby grew tired of firing pretend cannonballs, so the three of them headed for the gazebo. Katy was dancing in the middle and singing quietly.

She stopped when she saw the three of them. "This is just like in *The Sound of Music.* You know, when the older sister was dancing with the boy who delivered the telegram."

"You're too young to have a boyfriend," Bobby said.

"That's why I was dancing by myself," she said. "Besides, boys are silly."

"You'll change your mind about that some day," Jennifer said with a chuckle. "Let's walk down to White Point Gardens and I'll tell you a true story that I think you're going to like, Bobby."

As they walked she explained that the garden got its name from the piles of bleached oyster shells that were found there.

"That's not such a great story," Bobby said.

"How about this one?" she said. "You might remember that pirates were around in the 1700s and some of them visited Charleston. One of them was captured, tried and hung right here with more than 20 of his men."

"Ewwww," Katy said.

"It happened right here?" Bobby asked, suddenly interested.

"That's right," Jennifer said. "And...they left their bodies hanging here for quite awhile to send a message to other pirates."

"Now that's gruesome," Bobby said. "I wonder if their ghosts still haunt this place."

"I don't know if there are any ghosts here, but they say there are some in the Provost Dungeon just up the street. Want to go take a tour of it?"

"Yeah, that would be cool."

"Why don't you and Joey take the tour and Katy and I will check out some of these beautiful antebellum houses. Joey, is that okay with you?"

"Sure. Sounds like a plan," he said.

"Then off to the dungeon," Jennifer said.

Chapter 16
The Provost Dungeon

Jennifer paid for two tickets for the boys to take the next tour at the Old Exchange and Provost Dungeon. They had about 20 minutes before their tour was to begin, so she and Katy stayed with the boys until it was time to start. They walked through the gift shop and took advantage of the opportunity to visit the rest rooms which were located on the second floor.

Before going back downstairs they peeked into a large room that looked like a ballroom. It had light blue walls, shiny wooden floors, and large white columns that encircled the room. A sign said it was the Great Hall.

"Oh, it's so pretty," Katy said.

"George Washington visited Charleston while he was president. The people of Charleston held several banquets and balls in his honor. Some say he danced in this very room," Jennifer said.

Katy tiptoed into the center of the room, did a quick

pirouette, and then ran back out.

"I danced where George Washington danced," she said with a giggle.

"Way to go, Katy," Joey said, and gave her a high-five.

Jennifer checked her watch and said they needed to go to the bottom floor to start their tour. She told the boys she and Katy would meet them back in the main lobby when their tour was over.

"If we're not there when you're finished, just stay in the building. We might have trouble finding a parking space. They have some exhibits on the first floor. You can wander through them."

The boys took the elevator down to the basement. They were greeted by a man who looked like he had just stepped out of a history book. He wore a green vest and matching pants, a white shirt with billowy sleeves and topped it off with a tri-corn hat. About eight other people were standing in front of a heavy wooden door waiting for the tour to begin.

"I bet I know where that goes," Bobby said, pointing to the door.

"Duh! We're on the bottom floor and we're taking a tour of the Provost Dungeon. You think it could be the dungeon?" Joey said sarcastically.

The man in the costume moved toward the door and beckoned them to enter. They walked into a darkened space. Their guide told them this current structure was built on a site that was previously occupied by the Half-Moon Battery. He showed them a section of the original seawall of that building.

"What was the Half-Moon Battery?" a lady asked.

"It was the original fortification for the city of Charles Town. It was shaped like a half-moon and extended out into the water. Behind it stood a watch tower and the armory where weapons were stored," he said.

He told them in 1768 foundations were laid for the current Exchange to provide a place for businessmen involved in the import and export trade to conduct business. This location was ideal because it was at the center of the waterfront and at the end of one of the busiest commercial streets in Charleston.

The guide then directed them to their second stop where a robotic gentleman sitting at a work table described the kinds of activities that took place at the Exchange. A bright red parrot sat on a perch next to him adding its own comments and squawks.

"They're just like the animatronic characters we see at Disney World," Joey whispered to Bobby.

Across from that exhibit was a prison cell showing forlorn prisoners awaiting their fate. The tourists learned that pirates, including the infamous Blackbeard, were often a problem for this bustling port. They would attack vessels entering and leaving the harbor. When pirates were captured, many of them were imprisoned in the Guard House of the Half-Moon Battery, the tour guide told them.

He also told them about one particular pirate named Stede Bonnet who was known as the Gentleman Pirate because he came from a good family and was well-educated. He outfitted his ship and crew with his own money and served as one of Blackbeard's captains. But in 1718, he was

captured. He escaped once, but was recaptured, tried and sentenced to hang. He and some of his crew were hung at White Point Gardens just down the road from here, he said.

Bobby elbowed Joey and commented that the guide didn't tell them they were left hanging there for a long time. Joey told him not to say anything to the guide because it would be rude.

The tour moved on to another room where the guide described Charleston's version of the Boston Tea Party. The citizens of Charleston seized a shipment of tea as a protest to England for the tax they were expected to pay on it. The tea was stored right here in the Old Exchange for several years. Ironically, they later sold it to raise funds to fight the British during the American Revolution.

"It was actually from the steps of this building that the South Carolina General Assembly publicly read its constitution, declaring its 'unhappy differences' with Great Britain in 1776," he said. "However, in 1780 the British captured Charleston and controlled it until the end of the war."

Then he chuckled and told them one more piece of interesting history.

"The colonists hid a large stash of gun powder in a secret room in this basement," he said and pointed to the far wall. "Even though the British occupied this building after they captured the city, they never found the hidden gun powder."

Bobby raised his hand to ask a question. "Are there any ghosts here in the dungeon?"

The guide said there are many stories about the ghosts of people who had been imprisoned there – pirates and even some of the South Carolina patriots who were arrested during the British occupation. He said he had never seen any ghosts, but he had heard stories from some of the other people who worked there.

"That's what everyone says," Bobby said to Joey. "No one will tell me they have actually seen a ghost. They always say they know of other people who have seen them."

He asked Joey to take some pictures before they went upstairs, then they walked through the displays on the first floor. They learned it was a group of ladies who saved this building from being sold in the early 1900s.

"Katy's going to love this," Joey said. "I think all these stories about feisty ladies are going to make a big impression on our little sister."

"Yeah, we may be reading about her in the history books some day," Bobby said.

"Actually, that would be kinda cool."

"I guess we'd better be careful how we treat her," Bobby said. "When they do her life story on TV, we don't want to look like jerks."

"We will be jerks if we keep them waiting for us in this heat. Let's go."

Chapter 17
Home Sweet Home

While the boys were taking their tour, Jennifer wanted to show Katy some of the classic Charleston homes. She drove south on Bay Street and slowed down when they came to a row of yellow, blue and pink houses.

"This is called Rainbow Row and it's one of the most recognized places in Charleston," she told Katy. "This used to be a part of the waterfront district with lots of commercial activity in the 1700s. Merchants had their stores on the first floor, and lived above them on the second floor.

"Like so many other stories you've heard these past two days, these buildings were scheduled to be destroyed, but were saved by a woman named Dorothy Legge in the 1930s. Extensive renovations were done on them and now they're one of the most photographed places in the city."

"Another feisty woman," Katy said. "I want to be like that when I grow up."

"Oh, I have no doubt you will be," her mother said with

a smile.

By slowing down to look at the colorful row of houses, they were causing a small traffic jam. They continued south toward the Battery, but this time they were looking at the huge mansions along the waterfront. Many of them were three stories tall with long porches on each level.

"Those porches are called piazzas. Remember, we saw a house like that in Savannah," Jennifer explained. "They're built that way to keep the house cool. The houses were narrow, often only one-room wide, making it easy for the breezes to flow through the house.

"They also say in the early years the buildings were taxed by the length of the house along the street, so they built their homes very narrow and long."

They turned onto Battery Street to look at some of the huge mansions located across the street from the park. Most of them had wide porches with tall white columns facing the park. Green hedges and sometimes walls bordered the sidewalk, providing some privacy to the residents. Huge oak trees spread their branches over the front yards and the cars parked along the street.

"They call this section Battery Row," Jennifer said. "These homes received a lot of damage during Hurricane Hugo."

"I don't think I'd like to live here when a hurricane comes," Katy said.

"I understand, but many of these homes belong to families who have lived in them for generations. It would be hard to leave such a beautiful and historic home."

They drove up and down some of the side streets, pointing out special features to each other. Many of the houses had decorative ironwork on their doors and gates, shutters accenting their windows, and flowerboxes overflowing with colorful blossoms. Some had courtyards with fountains and beautifully landscaped gardens.

"They offer tours of some of these historic houses. I'd like to take one some day," Jennifer said.

"Me, too," Katy said. "We'll leave the boys at home."

"Speaking of the boys, we'd better get back to them. Their tour should just about be over."

"Are you sure we don't want to leave the boys there?" Katy said with a twinkle in her eye.

"Nah, we'd miss them after awhile," her mother said. "Besides, who's going to help you build your sand castle?"

"You're right," Katy said. "Sometimes brothers do come in handy. Let's go get 'em."

Chapter 18
Pawleys Island

Before leaving Charleston they stopped at the Old City Market so the kids could do some souvenir shopping. Katy bought an inexpensive bracelet; Joey bought a book that had information on the *Hunley* submarine; and Bobby bought some roasted almonds from one of the vendors.

"I'm saving my money for fishing tackle," he said. "I'm going to do some serious fishing when we get to the beach."

Jennifer bought a cookbook that contained a recipe for Shrimp and Grits. They stopped to watch some of the African-American ladies who were making and selling sweet grass baskets. Katy asked one of them how she learned to do that.

"I learned it from my grandmother, who learned it from her grandmother," she said. "It's an old Gullah tradition."

She continued to work on a tightly wrapped coil of sweet grass as she explained to Katy that it was an art form brought there by their ancestors who were slaves from West Africa.

"It's a large part of our history. We want to honor the tradition and our heritage."

"They're beautiful," Katy said. She knelt down to admire some that were spread out in front of the woman. There were many shapes and sizes in a variety of designs. They watched for several minutes more as the woman continued to weave.

"Why do they call it sweet grass?" Bobby asked.

"Because the grass commonly has a nice fragrance, kinda like fresh hay," the basket weaver said.

"What are they made of?" Joey asked.

"All natural materials – pine straw, marsh grass and palmettos. They were originally designed for 'fanning' rice to clean it, but they were also used for carrying or storing things like fruits and vegetables or sewing items," she said.

"Mom, can we buy one?" Katy said. "It will always remind us of Charleston."

"Sure," she said. "Why don't you pick one out?"

After many minutes of trying to decide, Katy finally selected a bowl-shaped one she said they could use as a bread basket. Jennifer selected another one for their grandparents and paid the woman. They eased their way back through the crowds of tourists in the market.

"There's so much more to see. We haven't done justice to this city, but it's time to move on," Jennifer said. "We'll just have to come back again."

When they got back to the mini-van, Jennifer asked Joey to sit in the front seat to help her navigate their way back to Highway 17. Before long, they were crossing the Cooper River Bridge which gave them a birds-eye view of the harbor. They stopped for lunch in Mount Pleasant and then journeyed on to Pawleys Island.

They saw many roadside stands selling sweet grass baskets along the highway. Soon they were back into rural

© iStockphoto

landscapes and thick forests. Katy again fell asleep in the back seat. Bobby nodded off too, but would never admit it.

They crossed the Waccamaw River after passing through Georgetown. Joey commented on the number of rivers they crossed. Jennifer told him this region used to have a lot of rice fields along its streams and swamps. "Cultivating rice required plenty of water," she said.

"The plantations developed an elaborate irrigation system of ditches and dams, utilizing the tidal flows from the swamps and streams. They also took advantage of the knowledge of the slaves who were brought here from the rice-growing regions of West Africa. The slaves played a critical role in the economic success of South Carolina, making it one of the richest colonies in North America," she said.

"So rice did for South Carolina what cotton did for Savannah," Joey said.

"Exactly," she said. "You can see why I think of traveling as a learning experience. I hope this trip helps you understand our country's history better."

As they got closer to Pawleys Island, Joey asked his mother if she had been there before.

"No, but I hear it's very laid-back and has a beautiful beach," she said. "The plantation owners used to bring their families here during the summer months to escape the heat and threat of malaria from the mosquitoes."

"I bet it was a lot cooler near the ocean," Joey said. "I don't know how they could stand it without air conditioning."

She asked him to read the directions her friend Deborah had given her so they could get to the island. As they crossed the causeway, they saw beautiful salt marshes on both sides of the road. Several people were fishing from docks that extended in the waterway.

"Wake up, Bobby. Looks like you've gotten your wish if you plan to do some fishing while we're here," Joey said.

Bobby sat upright, looking out both sides of the van. "Wow, this is great! I wanna go fishing right away."

"Hold on," his mother said. "We'll have to find someone who knows something about this area and get some advice about the fishing."

"Aw right, I hear you," he said. Then he nudged Katy to wake up.

"And under no circumstances are any of you to go off on your own. We're going to have some rules while we're here. We'll discuss all that as soon as we get settled."

Then she asked Joey to check the directions to the house where they'd be staying. At first they went the wrong way. But the island was less than 4 miles long with one main road, so it was hard to get lost. Most of the homes on the island were vacation rentals and were raised on heavy wooden pilings.

"Why are all of the houses up in the air?" Katy said.

Jennifer explained that they build them that way. When a hurricane or a bad storm comes through here, they can get a storm surge from the ocean. With the houses up off the ground, the water passes underneath them. Because this is an island, there's water on both sides of the houses, making them very vulnerable to flooding.

"That's very smart," Katy said. "Plus it helps keep some of the sand out of the house. You know, like those homes

in Savannah where they had the entrances on the second floor."

Joey smiled at his mother. "That's right, sweetie," she said.

"Here we are," Joey said. "It's that 2-story grey one with the white trim around the windows. Or would that be called a 3-story because of the space underneath it? Whatever."

Jennifer pulled the van under the house. There were stairs that led to a wide porch across the front facing the ocean. Bright-colored wooden chairs and plastic beach toys were scattered across the porch. A rope hammock was stretched across the far end.

"I've got to go next door to the neighbors to get the key," she said. "You kids stay here and I'll be right back. Did you hear me, Bobby? Stay on the porch."

"Yes, ma'am," he replied, and saluted.

Jennifer walked across a sandy driveway to a house that looked very similar to the one where they were staying. She knocked on the door and an attractive African-American woman answered.

"Hello, I'm Jennifer Johnson. Are you Mrs. Taylor?" she said.

"I am. But call me Caroline. Welcome to Pawleys Island. We've been expecting you," the woman said. "Won't you come in?"

"Actually I need to get back over there. I left the kids alone and I haven't laid down the ground rules yet."

"Oh, I know exactly what you mean. I have a 10-year-old who needs lots of rules."

"Is your 10-year-old a boy or a girl?"

"He's a boy, and he's all boy!"

"That's great. I have a 10-year-old too. Does yours like to fish?"

"He loves to fish, but right now crabbing is what's got his attention."

"Oh, I'm sure Bobby will want to meet him."

"Why don't you come over for dinner this evening? We're just roasting hot dogs and it will give the kids a chance to get to know each other."

"Sounds great. Although there are four of us. I'm a single parent, but I also have a 14-year-old son and a 5-year-old daughter," Jennifer said.

"That's fine. The more, the merrier," she said.

"What can I bring? We're going to the store to get some groceries, so please let me contribute something to the meal."

"If you could pick up some kind of dessert that would be great. I think I've got everything else," she said. "We often share meals with Deborah and her family."

"My kids will love it. We've been doing lots of touring and sightseeing these past two days and I think they'd welcome some other company besides their mother's."

Caroline told her they'd eat about 6:30, but to come over whenever they felt like it. She said her kids would welcome some new friends too.

When Jennifer returned to the house, the kids were playing a game of Crazy Eights with a deck of cards they had found on one of the porch tables.

"This place is so cool," Bobby said. "When can we go down to the beach?"

"Let's unload the car first, and then we'll take a peek at the beach. But we've got to go to the store to stock up on some food for the next few days," she said. "We've been invited next door for dinner, and guess what? The Taylors have a 10-year-old boy who likes to fish."

"I like this place already," Bobby said. "C'mon, let's get the car unloaded. I've got places to go, people to see, and fish to catch."

Chapter 19
A Miracle

The Johnson kids and the Taylor kids got along famous
ly. In addition to 10-year-old Michael, they had a 12-year-
old daughter named Elizabeth. Katy became immediately
infatuated with her and followed her everywhere. Fortu-
nately, Elizabeth was very flattered by the attention.

After they roasted hot dogs in a fire pit in front of the
Taylors' house, they took a leisurely walk on the beach. The
kids ran ahead, looking for shells and scampering in and
out of the ankle-deep waves, while the two ladies trailed
behind.

"It's just a matter of time before Bobby gets his clothes
wet," Jennifer said. "I can predict that with certainly."

"Oh, I can see he and Michael are going to be two
of a kind," Caroline said. "It seems half of my laundry is
Michael's clothes. That boy can get dirty just sitting in a
chair."

"They'll have a good time together, I'm sure," Jennifer

said. "Do you let him go fishing by himself?"

"No. He's not supposed to," she said. "His father will be driving down tomorrow and he can take both boys out fishing in the afternoon. We live in Charlotte, so he usually gets here after lunchtime."

She explained that her husband was an attorney and involved with a big case so he hadn't been able to spend as much time at their beach place as he usually does. "He tries to join us on the weekends," she said.

"So you own this place?" Jennifer asked.

"Yes, we bought it several years ago. We figured we wouldn't be doing a lot of traveling while the kids were young, so this would be an ideal getaway for us. It's really worked out well. We invite other family members to join us throughout the summer which is a great way to stay in touch with them."

"How wonderful," Jennifer said. "It's sad today that so many families are spread all over the country. The kids never get to know their aunts and uncles and cousins. And if you're divorced like me, it gets even more challenging."

They walked on a while longer, enjoying each other's company while keeping their kids in sight. Because it was getting dark, Jennifer whistled for the kids to come back. Elizabeth and Katy came running, excitedly telling them a big turtle had crawled up from the surf and was digging a hole near the sand dunes.

"Come quickly," Elizabeth said. "I think she's going to lay some eggs."

The ladies and girls went running to where the boys were standing. A man wearing a t-shirt with a sea turtle on it was motioning them to stay back. He slowly walked over to them, making a wide circle around the nesting turtle. He told them the turtle would abandon the nest if she became scared and lots of movement could scare her.

"She's a big loggerhead, about 250 pounds I'd say. She's using her rear flippers to dig the nest," he explained. "Once she starts laying her eggs, we can move around behind her and you can watch a miracle happen."

The kids were spellbound. Joey quietly told him they had visited the Georgia Sea Turtle Center on Jekyll Island earlier in the summer.

"We learned all about them and saw how some of the injured turtles were being treated and rehabilitated. But we didn't see anything like this," he said.

"You're very lucky. Not many people do," the man said. "I saw her crawling up the beach from my porch. We keep binoculars there so we can keep an eye out for 'em. I patrol the beach every morning from May through October looking for fresh nests. I'm a trained volunteer so I know what signs to look for. I've never had one dig a nest right in front of my house though. This is one for the record book."

When she had finished digging, she started laying her eggs. The man beckoned the kids to quietly move around behind her. They watched as dozens of ping-pong ball size eggs were dropped into the soft sand. Katy said she wished they had a camera, but the man said that a flash would upset the turtle.

"We ask people not to bring flashlights on the beach at night, and to turn off their lights after 10:00 PM if they live along the ocean. That's in case there are some hatchings that are beginning their journey to the water. They will go toward the light, thinking it's the moon or stars being reflected on the water."

After another 10 minutes, Jennifer said they should head back, as it was getting pretty dark.

"We'll check on the nest tomorrow," she said.

The man told them he'd be putting some mesh screens around the nest to protect it from predators and some do not disturb signs to warn people to stay away.

"If you see anyone messing with this nest, you come get me," he said. "I live right up there in the blue house."

The kids thanked him for letting them watch and slowly moved away. When they got out of hearing distance, Bobby jumped up in the air and let out a "Whoop!"

"That was so cool. I can't wait to tell Grandma and Grandpa about that," he said.

"Can we call them when we get back?"

"Well, it is getting kind of late. How about we give them a call in the morning?"

"OK, but I get to tell them because it was my idea to call," he said.

"No problem," Joey said. "We'll take some pictures of the nest tomorrow when it's daylight and we won't need a flash. We can e-mail them to Grandma on Mom's laptop."

When they got back to their house, they said their goodbyes and thanks for dinner.

"This is my favorite vacation so far," Katy said, as they walked up the steps to the beach house.

"Katy, this is your only vacation so far," Joey reminded her.

"So?" she replied. "It's still my favorite."

"You're right. This will be one for our record books," he said, and they went inside and closed the door.

Chapter 20
The Beach House

The next morning Jennifer was enjoying a cup of tea on the front porch when Joey joined her. He wore a Boston Red Sox t-shirt and athletic shorts which he used for pajamas.

"You're up early," she said.

"Yeah, I woke up and couldn't get back to sleep, so I thought I'd get up and read. I've got one more book to finish on my summer reading list before school starts."

"Are you excited about starting high school?" she asked.

"Yeah, but I'm also a little nervous. I'm looking forward to my classes, but I hear the seniors like to harass the freshmen."

"You'll do fine," his mother said. "Most of the time they're just having some fun. Of course, occasionally you run into a bully who can be just plain mean. If that happens, you report it."

"I think I'd rather just avoid them," he said.

"Joey, you can't avoid or ignore really bad behavior. It can be dangerous. If you run into any of that, I want you to tell me about it. And then we'll decide together what to do about it."

Joey was quiet and spread some sand around on the floor with his bare feet. When he looked up again, his mother was smiling at him.

"It will be all right, I promise you," she said.

"Easy for you to say. You've already lived through it."

"Yes, and I loved high school. I was elected to the student council and was on the swimming team. It was a great time for me, and it can be for you too. You just need to go into it with the right attitude."

"Right now I'm going to go into the kitchen and get some breakfast," he replied.

"How about some pancakes? We'll all need a big breakfast if we're going to spend the morning on the beach. You can help by frying some bacon. That should wake up the troops. There's nothing like the smell of frying bacon to get someone's attention in the morning."

Jennifer rummaged around the kitchen, looking for two frying pans and a bowl for mixing the pancake batter. After Joey brushed his teeth and put on a different t-shirt and his swimming trunks, he offered to help.

"Looks like you're ready to take a dip," she said.

"Be prepared," he said. "That's my motto."

Jennifer turned on the TV to catch the morning news and weather report while she was cooking. The house had a well-equipped kitchen, a dining area with a great view of the beach, and a spacious living room. It was decorated with shells, sea turtles, pelicans and colorful fish. The couch and chairs in the living room had blue slip covers on them, making it a very family-friendly room.

Jennifer was right about the smell of frying bacon. Soon Bobby stumbled out of the bedroom he was sharing with Joey, and Katy followed a few minutes later clutching her favorite teddy bear.

"Can I go see if Michael is up yet?" Bobby said.

"No, you're going to eat some breakfast and then we'll all go down to the beach. I'm sure he'll find you when he gets up."

"But I want to go fishing, and I hear the fish really like to bite early in the morning."

"You can go this afternoon when Michael's dad gets here. Caroline said he'd take both of you fishing after lunch."

"OK," he said dejectedly.

Over breakfast they discussed the turtle nest and were

guessing how many eggs they thought were in it. Bobby called their grandparents to tell them about the turtle nest. When Bobby was finished talking, Katy told them about the beautiful houses they saw in Savannah and Charleston and the bracelet she bought. Joey told his grandfather he bought a book that told about a famous submarine and he'd show it to him when they got home. He also told them he was taking lots of pictures. Then Jennifer asked about Max who seemed to be doing fine.

After they hung up, she told the kids she thought they should go to the beach in the morning, and then stay out of the afternoon sun their first day there.

"We don't want to get too sunburned," she said. "I want all of you to wear lots of sunscreen while you're outside. We'll try to find some indoor activities during the hottest part of the day."

"You can't catch fish indoors," Bobby complained.

"I understand. I'll talk to Mr. Taylor and make sure you're covered appropriately. He may not want to go fishing until later in the afternoon anyway."

The kids helped clear the table and Jennifer loaded the dishwasher. She packed some cold drinks in a small cooler while everyone changed into their bathing suits, except Joey. He rounded up some beach chairs and filled a canvas beach bag with plastic toys. There were buckets of different sizes, several shovels and scoops, and two Frisbees.

"I wanna make a really big castle," Katy said, as her mother lathered her with sunscreen. "I get to design it, but everyone can help me build it."

"Sounds like we already have a feisty female in our family," Bobby said to Joey.

"Ah, correction. Three feisty females," Joey said. "Don't forget about Mom and Grandma."

"You're right," Bobby said. "We don't stand a chance!"

Chapter 21
The Beach

Michael joined the Johnsons just as they were setting up their beach chairs on the beach.

"I saw you walking down to the beach, but my mom said I had to eat breakfast first," he said.

"Yeah, I understand. We had to eat too," Bobby said. "Wanna go in the water?"

"Sure. My mom said I could go into the water as long as there was an adult with us, and to ask your mom if it was okay," he replied.

"I'm sure it is, but let's go ask her," Bobby said.

Jennifer gave the boys permission and walked down to the water's edge with Katy. Joey played with his sister for awhile, looking for shells and chasing little fish. Then he joined the boys who were trying to jump over the waves as they rolled in. They continued this activity until Bobby swallowed a mouthful of ocean water when he dove into a large wave. He came up sputtering and coughing.

"I gotta get something to drink. This salt water is nasty," Bobby said.

"Last one to the blanket is a rotten egg," Michael said.

They charged toward the beach, splashing water everywhere. Katy scolded them for spraying water on her as they raced by.

"We should have left you in the dungeon," she yelled.

Jennifer gave each of them a juice box and asked Joey to take one to his sister. When they finished, she suggested they help Katy with her castle.

"That's girl stuff," Bobby said. "Building castles is no fun."

"Then you make it fun," she said. "Katy's been looking forward to this all week. I'd appreciate it if you'd go help her. It's her vacation too."

Joey was already building a base for the castle in the center of a large circle he had dug with a shovel. Katy was molding a wall around the outside with her hands. When Bobby and Michael offered to help, Katy handed them buckets and told them to go get some moist sand.

Elizabeth joined them and soon they were all busy adding their own individual touches to their sandy creation. As the castle began to take shape, their excitement grew.

"Let's do another one," Michael said. And so the

construction began on castle number two. This one was more elaborate and easier to build because they were "experienced", as Bobby put it.

When they were finished, they stood back and admired it. Joey went to get his camera so he could take a picture of it. He shot several pictures – some of just the castle, and some with the construction crew behind it. We'll have to send copies of these to Grandma with the ones of the turtle nest.

"How's the nest today?" Elizabeth asked.

"We don't know. We haven't gone down there yet," Joey said. "Mom, can we go check on the nest? I want to take

© iStockphoto

123

some pictures."

"Sure, let me grab my sun hat." And off they went.

The man who told them about the turtles was right. There was a mesh fence around it with signs warning people not to disturb it. Joey took several pictures. They could still see some of the tracks the turtle had made as she crawled out of the ocean and then back again, but many of them had been erased by the footprints of curious beach-goers.

"I wish we could see them hatch," Katy said.

"That will take about 6-8 weeks and we won't be here," Jennifer said.

"We won't be here either," Elizabeth said sadly.

"Perhaps we can ask that man in the blue house to let us know when they hatch," Joey said. "At least we'll know if they made it."

"That's a great idea," Jennifer said. "I'll go talk to him before we leave and give him our phone number. I'm sure he'll be happy to do that."

She told them it was getting close to lunch time and they needed to go back. But none of the kids seemed anxious to leave. They walked around the nest site several times, examining it from all angles.

"Kids, they're not going to hatch any time soon. We

can check on them again tomorrow. We need to head back. C'mon."

They left one at a time with each one giving it one last look.

"Nobody better mess with that nest," Michael said.

"Yeah," Bobby said. "That's our nest, and nobody messes with our nest."

Chapter 22
Going Crabbing

After a lunch of tuna fish sandwiches, Katy took a nap. Joey was reading his book and making notes. Bobby turned on the TV but was mostly watching out the window for Michael's dad's car. When a black SUV pulled into their driveway and parked under the Taylors' house, Bobby jumped up and asked his mother if he could go over there.

Jennifer was working a crossword puzzle, and told him to calm down. "Give them some time together. He just got there and he probably hasn't had any lunch. I'm sure Michael will come get you when they're ready to go," she said.

Bobby went back to the couch and pouted. About 3 o'clock Michael came over and asked if he wanted to go crabbing.

"I'd love to, but I've never been crabbing before," he said.

"We'll show you. C'mon." And then he added, "Make

sure you wear some old tennis shoes, ones with laces."

"Why do they have to have laces?" Bobby asked.

"You'll see," was all Michael said.

Jennifer made him put more sunscreen on and wear a baseball cap. She walked over to the Taylors' house with Bobby to introduce herself to Michael's father. He was a tall man with a friendly smile. She heard Bobby ask Michael if his dad played sports. Michael told him his dad had played basketball in high school and they often shot baskets together at home, but now he liked to play golf.

"I hope I'm as tall as he is when I grow up," Michael said.

Mr. Taylor said they'd be back in time for dinner. He found an old ice chest in the storage room under the house, and grabbed a tackle box, a fish net and a folding lawn chair. As they got into his car, he told the boys they needed to stop at the store first to pick up some chicken.

"Are we going to cook or fish?" Bobby asked Michael.

"Oh, we're going crabbing, all right. You just wait and see."

They went to a small store across the causeway that sold food and carried all kinds of fishing tackle. Mr. Taylor bought the boys a cold drink and let them each pick out a candy bar.

"Don't tell your mother about the candy bar. She'll read me the riot act. We'll just keep this our little secret," he said with a wink. Michael told Bobby that he and his dad had lots of little secrets like this when they were by themselves.

"Once we bought some ice cream and ate it right out of the container. Just two spoons and us. Women just don't understand," he said, quoting his father.

They drove back on the island and his father parked next to a dock that reached out into the marsh. He told them it belonged to a friend who said he could use it anytime he wanted. He handed the ice chest to Bobby and threw some heavy string and weights in it. Michael carried the tackle box and the net and his dad grabbed the lawn chair and the package from the store.

As they walked to the end of the dock, the no-see-ums started attacking them. Mr. Taylor set down the chair and pulled some bug repellent out of the shopping bag. He sprayed both the boys and then himself.

"Okay, gentlemen. We've got a few rules. First, try to stay on the dock. The goal is for us to catch some crabs, not for me to fish you out of the water. Second, stay out of that mud over there along the bank. It's pluff mud and it's very mushy. You're liable to sink in up to your knees if you go there. Pulling you out will be very difficult and you'll probably lose your shoes in the process."

"That's why I told you to wear shoes with laces. I learned that the hard way," Michael said. "You don't want to get into that stuff. It stinks like rotten eggs!"

"Rule number three," his father said. "Please no screaming when you catch something. Part of the beauty of crabbing is the peacefulness of this place. Let's don't scare off the wildlife or alienate the neighbors. I've had some of my most relaxing moments at places like this. Just last year I saw a bald eagle not too far from here."

Michael was already attaching a chicken neck to a string.

"Do you think this has enough weight on it?" he asked his father.

His father told him to add one more weight to it because the current was pretty strong here. Then he prepared a line for Bobby. He told him crabs love chicken necks.

"When you feel a tug on the line, chances are you've got a crab on it, maybe two."

It seemed like Michael had just dropped his line in the water and he had a tug. He pulled the line up and there was a crab with brilliant blue claws dangling from the end.

"Hurry, get the net," he said.

His dad swung the net under his catch and then

carefully dropped the crab into the ice chest.

"That's a good size male blue crab," his father said. He tilted the cooler so Bobby could see the crab. "The males have the bright blue claws and they're called Jimmies. The females have orange tips on their claws. In either case, watch out for those claws. They will pinch and it can be very painful."

"Nice catch," Bobby said to Michael. "Now it's my turn."

He threw his line into the water and waited. He thought he felt a tug, but he wasn't sure. He asked Michael how he knew when he had a crab on it. Michael told him he'd learn after a few times what it felt like. Just then, Bobby felt a good tug, so he tugged back.

"Not too hard now, or you'll lose him," Mr. Taylor said.

When Bobby pulled up his line, he had two crabs on it.

"Wow! Look at that," he cried. Then he remembered about not being loud. He knew that would be a challenge for him, as he wasn't known for being quiet.

Mr. Taylor captured the two crabs with the net and dumped them into the cooler.

"This is way better than fishing," Bobby said. "I can't wait to show Joey what I caught."

The kids spent the next hour and a half crabbing, while Mr. Taylor sat in the lawn chair with the net across his lap. They usually took turns bringing in a catch, but sometimes both of them would snag a crab at the same time and Mr. Taylor had to hustle to net them both. A couple of times they lost a crab in mid-air, but Michael declared that he'd get it the next time.

When the ice chest was fairly full, Mr. Taylor announced it was time to go home.

"I told your mother we'd be back in a couple of hours. We'd better call it a day."

"Dad, can we do this again tomorrow?" Michael said.

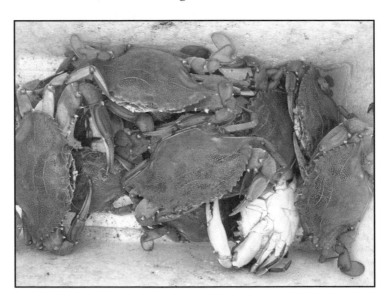

"We'll see. I've got a conference call at 3:00," he said. "I want you boys to remember that you never go fishing or crabbing alone. There are all kinds of things that can happen out here. Storms can come up pretty fast. Lightning is a real danger when you're near the water, and the tides are always changing. These tidal rivers are full of all kinds of marine life, and don't forget about the critters. There are turtles that can bite, poisonous snakes, and I've even seen an alligator in this water! You need to have a healthy respect for nature."

The boys helped pack up all the gear. As they were loading the car, clouds were rolling in from the ocean. A cool, moist breeze told them rain was on the way.

134

Chapter 23
Gullah Culture

After dinner, the kids went down to the beach to flatten out the castle they had made earlier. The rain had melted it down, but they still needed to level it out. Jennifer had found a brochure about sea turtles in the beach house. It said that all holes dug on the beach or sand castles should be leveled before dark. It explained that holes can become dangerous obstacles for sea turtles when they come up to lay their eggs or when the hatchings are struggling to get to the ocean.

As they were walking back to the house, they waved to the Taylors who were gathering around their fire pit. Caroline invited them over for s'mores.

"What's a s'more?" Katy said.

"Oh, you'll like them," Joey said. "First, you roast a marshmallow. Then you squeeze it between pieces of chocolate and graham crackers. The marshmallow gets gooey and the chocolate melts and it all mixes together. Um-mm.

It's an old camping treat."

When they joined the Taylors, Caroline introduced Jennifer and her kids to her Great-Aunt Bunny who was staying with them for the weekend. Bunny had a full head of white hair which contrasted with her copper-colored skin. She wore a bright orange and yellow dress with a chunky wooden bead necklace.

"Why do they call you Bunny?" Katy said. "Is that your real name?"

"Katy, don't be rude," Jennifer whispered.

"Oh, that's fine, child," she said. "Bunny is my Gullah name. The name on my birth certificate is Mary Elizabeth."

"Gullah," Joey said. "We heard that name in Charleston when we bought the sweet grass basket. What does Gullah mean?"

Caroline laughed and told the Johnsons they had opened a big door now. She said her aunt loved talking about Gullah history and warned them that she was a notorious story teller.

"My kids have grown up on her stories. And they're especially good by firelight," she said with a chuckle.

"Well, that's how we keep the culture alive," Aunt Bunny said in her defense.

"I wanna hear them," Katy said. "Please."

"Well first, let me answer this young man's question. The Gullah people are descendents of African slaves brought to this area to work on the rice plantations."

She told them the Gullah culture still exists in North Carolina, South Carolina, Georgia, and down to the northern tip of Florida. This culture includes distinct languages, foods, customs and art forms, like the making of sweet grass baskets.

"Our culture survived all these years because our people were so isolated. Many of them lived on the Sea Islands, and they had little contact with the outside world."

"So why do they call you Bunny, if your name is really Mary Elizabeth?" Katy asked again.

"A Gullah tradition was to give each child a pet name like a nickname, and they were often named after animals or things in nature. They tell me I moved like a rabbit, so I was named Bunny," she said.

She was quiet for awhile, staring into the fire. Caroline brought out a tray of marshmallows, Hershey bars and graham crackers. Michael produced five sticks he and his father had made from some long twigs. Soon the kids were roasting marshmallows, assembling their s'mores, and licking their fingers.

When they had eaten their fill, Elizabeth asked Aunt Bunny to tell them a story. Bunny thought for a moment, and then started telling a version of Br'er Rabbit. Bobby said he knew that story – that they had a book at home with that story in it. Aunt Bunny told him it was originally an African tale, and that's why she chose to tell it. She wanted them to see the connection between their cultures.

"We all borrow from each other," she said. "Our music, our foods, our stories. They eventually get mixed together. We all live on the same planet, so it only makes sense that our cultures would connect. Remember that the next time you see someone who looks different from you. You may discover that you have a lot more in common than you think you do."

When she realized the tone had gotten much too serious, she asked if they wanted to hear a ghost story. All the kids said yes immediately, even Katy, although she crawled up into her mother's lap.

"Tell us about the Grey Man," Michael said.

"Who's the Grey Man," Bobby said.

"Ah, the Grey Man," Aunt Bunny said. "Now that's a story!"

Chapter 24
The Grey Man

All eyes turned to Bunny. She took a deep breath, looked up in the sky, and then began. She told them there are several stories about the Grey Man, but the one heard most tells of a young man who had just returned from a long voyage and was anxious to see his sweetheart on Pawleys Island. In trying to get there quickly from Georgetown, he took a shortcut through a marshland. According to his servant who was following behind him, the man's carriage got stuck in some quicksand and sank, killing the young man.

Shortly after his funeral, his fiancé was walking on the beach on a windy day and saw his figure in front of her, warning her to leave the island. When she told her parents what she had seen, they left immediately. The next day a terrible hurricane destroyed many of the homes on the island, but their house was left undamaged.

"Since then, many people have reported seeing a man

in a long grey coat warning them to leave when storms are approaching. According to those who have heeded his warnings, when they return they find their homes safe while others around them have been destroyed," she said. "So they say anyone who sees him will come to no harm."

When Bunny finished, there was total silence. Finally Michael said, "I love that story. No matter how many times I hear it, I love it."

"Do you think there really is a Grey Man?" Bobby asked Bunny.

"I don't know, son," she answered. "But there are plenty of people who claim to have seen him."

"That's what I always hear," he said dejectedly. "I just want to see a ghost for myself some day."

Just then, the fire made a loud pop and they all jumped. When they realized what it was, they started laughing.

"On that note, I'm going to retire," Bunny said. "It's been a long day for me so I'm going to get some rest. I've enjoyed meeting all of you, and I look forward to seeing you again tomorrow. Good night," she said and got up to leave.

"Michael, please walk with Bunny to the house and up the stairs. It's dark and I don't want her to miss a step," Caroline said to her son.

Michael jumped up and offered her his arm. "Madam,

may I escort you?"

Bobby jumped up and offered his arm on her other side. "We'll protect you in case you run into any ghosts along the way."

"Speak for yourself," Michael said. "If I see a ghost, I'm running the other way – as fast as I can!"

They all laughed except Katy who was sound asleep in her mother's arms.

142

Chapter 25
Fun in the Sun

They spent the next morning on the beach. Katy and Elizabeth were building another castle, only this time they were making it with wet sand, dripping it into pointed towers. The boys were throwing a Frisbee back and forth, making up new games and challenging each other loudly. The adults, except for Aunt Bunny, were sitting under umbrellas discussing some of the latest news stories.

When Mr. Taylor jumped up and ran into the surf, the boys followed enthusiastically. They tried body surfing for awhile and then switched to a game of water tag using a beach ball. When they were finished playing in the surf, they were thirsty and tired.

"Are you boys ready for some lunch?" Caroline said.

"Not yet," Michael said. "We have to show Dad the turtle nest."

"Whoa, give me a minute, sport," his father said. "You guys wore me out. Let's rest a little, and then I'll go with you."

Katy and Elizabeth were putting the finishing touches on their castle. When they had finished, Katy asked Joey if he'd take a picture of it.

"I want a picture of this for my scrapbook. Mom said we could make one when we get home. I want to remember this trip forever," she said.

Joey agreed to photograph their creation and offered to e-mail some photos to Elizabeth too.

"You have very nice children," Caroline said.

"Why, thank you," Jennifer replied. "I think so too."

The ladies gathered up the chairs and blankets while the kids took Mr. Taylor to see the turtle nest.

"I'm taking Aunt Bunny and Elizabeth shopping later. Would you and Katy like to go with us?" Caroline said. "James will be here, working on some paperwork so the boys should be okay."

"I'm sure Katy will want to go. She adores Elizabeth. What time are you going? She usually takes a short nap after lunch."

"After all this sun, I may take a short nap after lunch too," Caroline said with a laugh. "How about 2:30? Does that work for you?"

"That's great. I'll go fix the kids some lunch. I have a

feeling they're going to be starving when they get back."

They trudged back up through the soft sand of the dunes and went their separate ways, agreeing to see each other a little later. Jennifer took a quick shower before the kids got back. Then she put a frozen pizza in the oven.

When the kids returned, Jennifer asked Katy if she wanted to go shopping later. Katy responded excitedly that she did. Jennifer asked the boys if they'd be all right by themselves.

"Mr. Taylor will be here if you need anything," she said. "Bobby, I imagine you're going to be spending time with Michael anyway.

"You betcha," he said.

"I'm just about finished with this book and then I've got to write a critique. May I use your laptop while you're gone?" Joey said.

"Of course. I think they have Wi-Fi if you want to check your e-mail too," she said with a wink. She knew Joey had been e-mailing his friend Barby in Boston, ever since they had met a year ago in St. Augustine when her family was there on vacation.

"Actually, they do. I already checked," he said. "I wanted to see the scores of last night's Red Sox game, and I sent an e-mail and some photos to Barby. She was very excited about the turtle nest."

Jennifer could tell he had something else on his mind, but she waited for him to share it.

"Speaking of Barby," he said cautiously, "she wants to know if we're going to come to Boston next summer."

"I'd love to go. It will just depend on what the family budget looks like then. Four plane tickets to Boston can be expensive. And then we'd need a rental car and meals."

Joey looked disappointed.

"But you never know. A lot can happen between now and next summer."

"Yeah, like I could win the lottery," Bobby said.

"You can't win the lottery," Joey said. "You have to buy a ticket and kids can't buy tickets."

"That doesn't matter. I'll get Grandpa to buy me one. And if I win the lottery, we'll all go to Boston. And New York. And Chicago. We'll just go everywhere," he said.

"Don't forget the Bahamas," Katy added. "You said you wanted to go to the islands to search for pirate buried treasure some day."

"Yeah, we'll go there too. I bet they have great fishing down there."

"Okay, dreamers. As soon as you finish your pizza, I want you to get cleaned up. Let Katy get her shower first so she can take a nap. I'm also going to do a load of laundry, so please get out all your dirty clothes."

"Hey, I thought we were on vacation," Bobby said. "Laundry is work."

"We are on vacation, but unfortunately the dirt and sand are not. I'll start a load as soon as everyone has showered. And speaking of work…Bobby, I'd like you to sweep the sand off the front porch."

"Aw, Mom. How come I have to do everything?"

"Well, if you'd like to trade places with your brother and write his critique for him, then I'm sure he'd be glad to sweep the porch."

"I'll sweep the porch," he said, and didn't say another word.

Chapter 26
Boys Will Be Boys

Joey was reading in the hammock on the front porch when Bobby, Katy and his mother walked over to the Taylors' house. Michael was watching TV when Bobby knocked on his bedroom door.

"This is boring," Michael said. "They won't let me bring any video games here. They say I need to enjoy the natural world while I'm here."

"I'd say fishing and crabbing are part of nature," Bobby said.

"Yeah, but my dad's waiting on a phone call. He said we might go out later."

They watched TV for awhile, but soon grew bored with it.

"Let's go outside and find something to do," Michael said. "I'll ask my dad again if he can take us crabbing."

But when they got downstairs, Mr. Taylor was on the phone. He waved at the boys, but was focused on his conversation. Michael indicated they were going outside, and his father shook his head in acknowledgment.

They walked to the end of the driveway and could see the marsh across the street. There was a car and a truck in the parking lot near a small sandy beach.

"Look at that. Those guys are fishing and we're over here with nothing to do. I wish we could be over there," Michael said.

"Yeah, but we can't go over there alone," Bobby said.

Michael grinned. "Actually, that's exactly what they said. We can't go fishing alone. But look, there are other people over there – we won't be alone."

Bobby thought about it for a minute. "Are you suggesting what I think you're suggesting?"

"Yep. Our moms won't be back for several hours. My dad will be on the phone for awhile. We could slip over there, catch a few crabs and be back before anyone misses us."

"What will we do with the crabs, and what will we use for bait?" Bobby said.

"We've got some bait left over from yesterday. My dad put it in the refrigerator so we could use it today. And we'll just turn the crabs loose. We'll keep track of who caught the most. C'mon, it will be fun, and no one will ever know."

Bobby hesitated, but when he looked across the street again, he knew he'd agree.

"We better not get caught. My mom will skin me alive," he said.

Michael went upstairs to get the chicken out of the refrigerator. His dad was still on the phone, pacing back and forth on their front porch as he talked. Bobby gathered up the lines and the net, and they ran across the road and positioned themselves behind some shrubs.

One man was fishing to the right of them, and they could hear voices off to their left where two ladies were crabbing off of one of the docks nearby. Michael explained that crabbing from the bank would be a little trickier, but he had done it before. They found a spot that stuck out into the water and baited both of their lines. Bobby felt the first tug, so Michael grabbed the fishing net and pulled in the first crab.

"Remember what my dad said about their claws. I've never been pinched, but I saw it happen to another kid once and it was not a pretty sight. The crab would not let go and the kid was screaming his head off."

"Then I'll let you handle the crabs, Mr. Experienced Crabber," Bobby said.

At first they had lots of activity, but then there was

nothing. The tide was changing and they figured that was causing the problem. Michael pointed to a small sand bar just across from where they were and suggested they wade out to it and try their luck.

"Watch your step. Put your feet where I step so you don't sink in."

They waded across a shallow area to get to the sand bar. As soon as they threw their lines out, they both caught crabs. Bobby's line had two blue crabs on it. They were laughing and having a good time and did not notice the grey clouds forming behind them or how fast the tide was rising.

A bolt of lightening got their attention. Remembering what his dad had said, Michael said they better go. They gathered their gear and scrambled to leave. They were shocked when they saw the place they had waded through earlier was now a rushing current. Drops of rain were starting to fall. The fisherman who had been fishing not far from them was gone. Another flash of lightening with a quick thunderclap made them both jump.

"What do we do?" Bobby yelled to Michael.

"I don't know. If we cross at the wrong spot, we could end up in the muck and that could be really bad."

The sand bar they were standing on was getting smaller

and smaller as the tide came in. The rain started to get much heavier. They could no longer see the road, although they could hear the cars going by.

"Maybe we could get someone's attention," Bobby said.

"If we can't see them, then they can't see us," Michael said. "We're going to have to cross somewhere – the question is where?"

As the water started covering their shoes, they looked around frantically, trying to figure which way to go. When another flash of lightening sliced through the air, Bobby noticed a figure standing on a dock across from them.

"Michael, did you see that?" he said.

"No, what?"

"I thought I saw someone over there," he pointed toward one of the docks. The rain let up a little and they both saw a man in a long coat pointing to their right.

They looked in that direction and saw a place where some marsh grass was peeking up through the water. The grass seemed to get thicker near a sandy bank that was opposite from where they had crossed before.

"What do you think?" Bobby said.

"We can't stay here. Let's go." He grabbed the net. "This might come in handy," he said.

"I'll go first, but hold on to the other end of the pole. If one of us trips or gets stuck in the mud, the other one can help him out."

When they stepped off the sand bar, the water quickly rose up to their waists. They cautiously stepped forward, aiming for the grassy area. At first it was fairly easy to walk through the water, but then they hit a mushy spot. It was like wading through wet cement.

"Michael, I can't get my foot out of the mud," Bobby said.

"Keep trying," Michael said. "Don't panic, just twist your foot and try to ease it out."

Michael took the handle end of the fish net and started digging around Bobby's shoe. After a few probes, his foot came loose.

"C'mon, let's get out of here," he said.

"Man, you were right. That stuff stinks!"

Within the next few steps, the ground became more solid. The water was becoming more shallow and they could see a sandy area in front of them.

"We're not home free yet," Michael said. "Be careful of that mud over there. It looks like it would like to swallow us both up."

When they reached some hard sand where the water

was only ankle deep, they ran the rest of the way. They threw themselves down on the bank and breathed heavily.

"That was scary," Bobby said. "I thought we were goners."

"What are we going to tell our parents?" Michael said.

"How 'bout the truth?"

"I dunno. My dad will never let me out of his sight after this."

As they stood up and examined their clothes and shoes, it occurred to them to go thank the man who had saved them.

"Who was that man?" Bobby said.

"I dunno. I've never seen him before."

"He looked…" Bobby paused. "He looked kinda unreal. You know what I mean."

"Yeah," Michael said. "Come to think of it, he was wearing a long coat. Why would someone wear a coat in this heat?"

They looked over to where they had seen him, but could not see the docks from where they were standing.

"Let's go see if he's still there," Bobby said.

They crawled up a sandy bank and walked through an opening in the bushes so they could get a better view of the waterfront. There was no sign of the man.

"Michael, are you thinking what I'm thinking?" Bobby said.

"Maybe he was just our imagination."

"Yeah, but we both saw him. And he saved our lives. Remember, Aunt Bunny said the Grey Man warned people and told them to leave when a storm was coming. Well, we were in danger; he warned us; and there was a storm."

"I dunno, Bobby. I guess we'll never know. We better go back and try to figure out what to do next."

When they got back to the house, they turned the garden hose on each other. They washed off the fishing net which was full of sand and put it back where it had been stored.

"You know, if we play our cards right, we might get away with this," Michael said.

"Nah, I'd die of the guilt," Bobby said. "I'm going to tell my mom, but I might wait until we get back home. If I tell her now, it will just ruin the rest of her vacation."

"Yeah, and yours too," Michael said. "I'll eventually tell my dad, but not right now. He's got a lot on his mind, and I don't want to be the one to ruin his weekend."

So they agreed to not confess right away. Bobby ran home, running up the stairs two steps at a time.

"What happened to you?" Joey said.

"Oh, Michael and I got into a mud fight. I better get cleaned up before Mom gets back."

"You'd better hurry. She called about ten minutes ago and they're on their way back."

Bobby took a quick shower, even shampooed his hair. Then he gathered his dirty clothes and put them in the washing machine. He asked Joey to help him get it started. Then he went to his bedroom and started to straighten it up. As Joey stuck his head in the door to tell him something, he startled Bobby who let out a yelp.

"What's the matter with you? You act like you saw a ghost," he said.

Bobby fell on the bed and grabbed his heart.

"You'll never know, big brother. You'll never know."

Chapter 27
All's Well that Ends Well

That evening both families went to a local restaurant for dinner. Michael and Bobby were especially quiet throughout the meal. Aunt Bunny kept looking at them closely.

"You boys act like you've got a secret," she said to them quietly.

The boys looked at each other, full of remorse and guilt.

"Aunt Bunny, have you ever done something really stupid?" Michael said.

She laughed out loud. "Of course, I have. Everyone has. That's a part of growing up."

"Well, let's just say we did a lot of growing up today," Michael said.

"I kind of sensed that something was going on. I had some very strange sensations during that rainstorm this afternoon. Did that have anything to do with it?"

"Yes, ma'am," he said in amazement.

"Well, all's well that ends well," she said. "Did you learn from it?

Both boys nodded.

"Then why don't we forget about it for now and enjoy a nice dinner. I hear the crab is delicious here," she said with a wink.

The boys looked at each other in shock.

"How did she know?" Bobby said later when they were riding back to the island.

"Aunt Bunny seems to know a lot of things that we can't explain."

"I know something else we can't explain, and it's going to drive me crazy."

The next day the Johnsons had to leave. They spent one last morning on the beach. Brown pelicans flew over their heads in a straight line while several dolphins were swimming just beyond the breakers. Katy squealed with delight every time one of them surfaced. Joey tried to take some pictures of them, but he was looking directly into the sun and wasn't sure they'd turn out.

"I'd love to get a picture of them to send to Barby in Boston," he told his mother. "She keeps e-mailing me about the whales they see up there. I'd like to show her some of our marine life."

Bobby and Michael were kicking a beach ball back and forth.

"Are you guys going to come back next summer?" Michael asked.

"I don't know. You'll have to ask my mom. Her friend invited us to use the beach house for the weekend. Maybe next year we can rent one ourselves.

"That would be cool." Michael said. "It's going to be boring when you leave."

They played awhile longer, than trotted down to the turtle nest for one last look. Jennifer talked to the turtle man, as they called him, and he agreed to let them know when the babies started to hatch.

"Maybe he can take some pictures for us," Katy said.

"I don't think so," Jennifer said. "I read where they usually hatch at night, and remember, he told us not to show any bright lights. So flash photography is out. We just have to hope that most of them make it to the ocean safely."

After they cleaned the house and loaded the car, they said their goodbyes to the Taylors. Elizabeth gave Katy a necklace with a small sea turtle charm. She said it was something to remind her of their trip to Pawleys Island. Katy gave her a big hug. Jennifer exchanged e-mail addresses with Caroline.

"We'd love to have you join us here next year," Caroline said. "We have plenty of room, and you're like family now."

Bobby and Katy looked pleadingly at Jennifer. "We'll see," she said. "It has been fun, and we didn't have any catastrophes."

Bobby looked at Michael and they both grinned.

"We'd better get on the road. We have a long ride ahead of us," Jennifer said.

The mothers hugged each other and then all of the kids. Bobby patted Michael on the back and said, "Later, dude."

"Oh wait, just a minute," Mr. Taylor said. He ran into the house and came back with a plastic bag in an insulated container.

"What's this?" Jennifer said.

"It's some of the crab meat from when the boys went crabbing the other day. I thought Bobby would enjoy eating it later and remembering his crabbing experience on Pawleys Island."

"Mr. Taylor, I can assure you I will never forget it!" Bobby said.

As they drove away, a man on the radio was saying they were expecting some severe thunderstorms that afternoon on Pawleys Island.

"It's a good thing we're leaving today," Jennifer said. "We wouldn't want to get caught in a storm."

"No, that would not be good," Bobby said. "It's time to go home."

THE END

About the Author

Jane R. Wood has always loved history. It started with her early years growing up in Astoria, Oregon, and continued when her family moved to Cocoa, Florida, near the Kennedy Space Center. She has lived in Northeast Florida for more than thirty years and enjoys exploring the historic and cultural heritage of Southern cities like Savannah and Charleston.

Her passion for writing began in the 4th grade during a poetry unit when she discovered the magic of words. Mrs. Wood has been a middle school and high school English teacher, a newspaper reporter and a television producer.

Jane Wood resides in Jacksonville, Florida, with her husband Terry, and is now a full-time writer of kids' books. You can learn more about Jane Wood and her books on her website at www.janewoodbooks.com.